NO EXIT

True 2 Life Street Series
Part 1

https://source self service 2
ceridian.com/
arbitron

No Exit

Al- Saadiq Banks

TRUE 2 LIFE PRODUCTIONS

No Exit

For information contact:
True 2 Life Productions
P.O. BOX 8722
Newark, N.J. 07108
E mail: true2lifeproductions@verizon.net

Author's email: alsaadiqbanks@aol.com

ISBN: 0-9740610-0-X

REVISED EDITION

Printed in Canada

INTRODUCTION

Welcome to Newark (Brick City) New Jersey. Home of some of the grimiest people you could ever meet. It's a tough place to live, and even a rougher place to visit.

If you don't believe me, open up the Newark Star Ledger (the local newspaper). On any given day you can read articles of petty car theft to gruesome stories of executioner style murder. Some murder as an occupation. Some murder just because. While others have to murder to protect themselves from all the above.

Newark is a place where children are introduced to the street life before they become teen-agers. A place where children are taught that fast money is the only money, and through the game they can attain all of their goals.

Everyone has a position to play in this game. Some take on the roles of kingpins. Some become lieutenants. While the majority will never be more than soldiers, others will take on the role of murderers.

How do you get in the game? That's easy. All you have to do is get in where you fit in. The question is; how do you get out of the game? The answer is, you don't.

There is NO EXIT!

This book is dedicated to my lovable daughter.
Fajr, despite what everybody says, "Daddy is not the bad guy."
Your big, beautiful eyes and your snagger toothed smile, is what
gave me the inspiration to make a change in my life.

I love you little mommy
Xoxoxo

CHAPTER 1

It's spring of 1989 at approximately 5:00 pm. The fellas are crowded around the 27" black and white television playing video games.

"Du, I've been beating you all day. You haven't won a game yet!" Tony shouts.

"I know; my mind isn't on this game shit. I got a lot going on," Du Drop explains.

"What kind of shit?" Tony asks.

"The same old shit man; that dough," Du Drop replies.

Nigga, you need a job!" Tony shouts.

"Yeah, alright!" says Du Drop.

"Fuck that working shit. That ain't hitting on shit!" E Boogie screams foolishly.

"I'm telling you. I need dough right now! Not next week, right now!" Du Drop affirms.

"Man, I'll be damn if I'll be running around here at twenty years old with no money in my pocket. I'll be working four jobs or something," says Tony.

Tony has just turned eighteen years old. He's the youngest of the three boys. E Boogie and Du Drop are both twenty years old.

"You're going to be a working motherfucker, while I'm sitting back lounging like a motherfucker," E Boogie says arrogantly.

"You aren't going to be doing too much lounging, selling that garbage ass weed you got. Somebody gonna fuck around and kill your ass; out there selling that rabbit food," Tony says jokingly.

"Yeah alright. Just keep flipping them burgers and

cleaning those pissy ass toilets, you nerd ass nigga. You'll be forty years old, with a tight ass uniform on, screaming, "Yes, can I take your order?"

"I bet you I won't be forty still working at fast food restaurants. By that time, I'll have a whole chain of them shits," Tony says defensively.

Tony is getting mad at E Boogie. You can see it all over his face. Tony is a bright young man, with a lot of ambition. At the present, he's in school and working part time, while E Boogie on the other hand is a small time weed hustler, with more mouth than money. The two boys always go back and forth at it about Tony working at the fast food restaurant.

"Man I'm out. I'm about to go sell some of this garbage ass weed," E Boogie says sarcastically, *as he counts a big stack of ones and fives. He's showing off for Tony. E is nothing but a showoff.* "Du, what are you going to do? Are you leaving with me, or are you staying here with the nerd?"

"I'm staying here for a little while."

"Alright, peace! Don't let burger man talk you into getting a job with him," E says, *as he laughs in Tony's face.*

"Get the fuck out!" Tony screams.

"Later!" E screams, *as he walks out the door.*

"Tony, shit getting crazy. This broke shit ain't working. I'm a grown ass man. I can't keep living like this. Look at me, I'm twenty years old and I'm not doing shit for myself."

Du is an all around good kid. He just lacks motivation. He's a high school drop out, and he never worked a day in his life.

"Well, do something for yourself than!"

"Something like what?" Du asks. "No disrespect but I can't do that fast food shit. That ain't for me. I respect the hell out of you for that, but I can't do it."

"What's the problem with it?"

"The whole shit, Tony. The tight ass suit, the tie and that fucked up hat."

"Well, I gotta do what I gotta do for right now; at least

until I graduate. Then hopefully I can get a better job."

"I don't know what to do. E keeps telling me to get down with him on that weed shit. At first I wasn't with it, but now it's sounding better and better each day. Yo, E stacking right now," Du claims.

"E ain't stacking shit. The mall is getting all his money. He's walking around here like a Polo mannequin."

"Hey man, that's his thing. That's what he lives for, clothes and bitches," Du replies.

"Listen Du, all I'm going to tell you is, E is a dumb motherfucker, and if you fuck with him long enough you're going to be a dumb motherfucker too. I mean I love E, but he don't see the big picture."

"What is the big picture? Is it working for forty-five years, and still ending up on welfare when you retire? Starving like a motherfucker, eating Vienna sausages or pork and beans for dinner, while these crackers living it up, going away to France and Switzerland. Tony there is no big picture. Our picture don't get no bigger than this black and white TV," says Du, *as he points to Tony's raggedy TV, which has a clothes hanger replacing the antenna.* "Don't let these motherfuckers fool you. You'll be flipping them burgers for the rest of your life."

"Never that!" Tony screams. "The picture gets as big as you make it. Du gotta do what Du need to do to get the fuck out the hood. Fuck them crackers, they already got theirs. They got old money from five generations back. You can't compare yourself to them. We're two broke ass niggas from the ghetto. We have to start from here, right from scratch."

"Yeah start from right here selling burgers; if we get lucky we can retire as managers," Du says sarcastically.

"I see there is no need to talk to you being that you already have your mind set," says Tony. "Do your thing, but when it's all over, I'll be sixty years old, in my backyard with my wife chilling, laid out on beach chairs eating watermelon. House fat as hell, while ya'll motherfuckers is still on that corner stuck on that dumb shit."

"I hope it all work out for you, but I really can't see it," says Du.

"You can't see it because you got your eyes and mind closed. You will never be able to see shit like that," Tony explains. "As for me, I'm going to continue this school shit and this work shit. And that other shit; I'll leave that up to them other niggas. I just hope the outcome is whatever the hell they're looking for."

"I hope so too," Du agrees. "So what are you doing tomorrow?"

"Tomorrow I have a college test to take, to see if I get accepted. Then from there I'm off to work."

"Alright, well I'm about to jet. I'll get with you later on this week," says Du.

"Alright then."

"Alright later baby," Du replies, *as he walks out the door sluggishly.*

Tony sits there envisioning his future as an older man, with a career and a family, living the AMERICAN DREAM. He isn't worried about his future. He's worried about Du Drop and E Boogie. Du being a high school drop out with no motivation, Tony knows Du can't make it like that in the real world. And as for E, the street life is all he knows. He has been standing on corners ever since he was nine years old.

CHAPTER 2

"Damn! Where's this joker?" E questions. "He said he would be here at 7:00. We can't be fucking around in this park. County Police will be making their rounds soon."

"Word up," Du Drop agrees. "Circle the block one time; if he's not here by then, we're out."

E continues to circle the block in the little raggedy Chevy Chevette. As they turn they notice a car approaching them. The driver is flashing the high beams. It's a candy apple red convertible Saab with tinted windows.

"Here's this motherfucker!" says E.

The car pulls up side by side with them. The driver's side window begins to roll down slowly. The passenger screams out, "park right here and take a ride with me."

As they're walking E begins to speak, "Du I have to warn you, this nigga is arrogant as hell. Don't let him piss you off. Just answer whatever questions he asks you and don't let the bullshit bother you."

"You got it," Du replies.

Once they're seated in the car the driver pulls off, while the passenger just sits there laid back in the seat with his feet on the dashboard. After riding for six or seven blocks the passenger finally speaks. "E, you got company huh?"

"Oh, this is my man Du Drop. We grew up together."

"Du Drop? What kind of name is that?" the passenger asks.

"We gave him that nickname back when we were kids. Ever since he was young, he's been knocking niggas out. He even knocked a few grown men out."

"Yeah that's cute and all, but I'm a grown motherfucker, and I carry a grown motherfucking gun," says the passenger, *in a low but assertive tone.*

The passenger reaches under the seat as he speaks. Finally he comes up with a big silver 44 magnum. It looks as if the barrel of the gun never ends. He points the gun at Du's chest. "If a punk ass young boy like you even think about knocking me the fuck out, I'll kill you and anybody who feels sorry for your young ass. Du Drop, huh?"

"Come on baby, chill. He don't want beef," E pleads.

"Well, what the fuck do he want? What is his purpose in here anyway?"

"He wants to get down with me. He got some people and I got some people. We're going to get together and get paid."

"Little nigga you ever clock before?"

"Nope," Du replies.

"Then how you know you cut out for this shit?"

"I can handle it, please just try me out," Du begs.

"I'll try you out, but if there's any bullshit, E will have to take the weight. You hear me E?"

"Yes."

"E, reach under your seat and grab that weed. That's 4 pounds in the bag. I want $800 a pound, which comes out to $3,200. Not $2,000, not $3,000. I want $3,200 back."

"Alright good looking out," says E. "I'll beep you as soon as we finish."

As they rode back to their car no one said a word. Once they got in their car Du finally spoke. "Your man is crazy as hell. What the fuck is wrong with him?"

"He's the man," E replies. "He thinks everybody is supposed to be scared of him. You know how it is."

"You scared of him!" shouts Du.

"You crazy as hell! I ain't scared of that punk motherfucker. I'm just playing my part. When I get in position, riding around in big cars and giving out work and shit, then I can tell him and a bunch of other people to kiss my ass."

"Enough of that punk ass nigga. How are we going to do this?" asks Du.

"You heard the man. He wants $3,200 back. We gotta get this money," Du replies. "Being that you're just getting started I'm only going to give you one pound. I'll take the other three. If I finish before you, I'll help you move yours. Then when you build your clientele up we can split the weed down the middle."

"That's cool," Du replies.

"Let's go to the smoke shop on South Orange Avenue, to get the empty bags. We can bag the weed up in my house."

After purchasing the empties, the two proceed to E's house.

"Go ahead up stairs, while I make sure nobody is home," says E.

"Alright!" Du replies.

Du starts walking up the stairs to E's room. He has never been inside E's room before. It's crazy. It looks like a Dr. Jay's sneaker store, nothing but wall-to-wall sneaker boxes. His room even has the new sneaker smell. His closet looks like a Macy's department store. He has Polo everything; even the sheets and pillowcases. "This nigga really know how to spend that money," Du blurts out.

E busts in the room. "Yo, my little brother was in the living room but I sent him outside. We'll be done before my moms get home. Light up the incense and put that tape in the radio."

They begin bagging up the weed. This is Du's first time so all he does is watch and listen to E's big dreams of one day becoming a drug kingpin.

Altogether they have been in the room for over three hours. E has been smoking the whole time.

"Finished, finally!" E shouts. "I'm tired as hell. Yo, pass me the air freshener. That weed got the room banging." *E begins spraying. He must have used half a can already.* "Du, you ready?"

"Yeah!"

"Don't forget your bag," says E.

Du grabs his weed and they proceed out the door, on their way to Du's house. After getting into E's car, E pulls out the E.Z. Wider and a bag of weed. He begins to roll a joint.

Finally, he lights the joint and drives off. After taking three pulls he passes the joint to Du. **"Here, take a pull."**

"Nah, I'm alright."

"Take a hit motherfucker! How are you going to know if the shit is any good?"

"I'll let you sample it," Du answers.

"I ain't no motherfucking test monkey! You better take a pull of this shit!"

Du reaches out hesitantly and he takes a small pull. **"Are you happy now?"**

E begins laughing. **"Boy, you a punk ass nigga, I swear.**

Du has never smoked before, so he doesn't know what to expect. He sits quietly for a second and then his vision gets blurry. He starts feeling dizzy. He doesn't want to complain to E because he doesn't want to sound like a chump. He just sits there quietly until they pull up to his house. **"Later E!"**

"Alright Du, I'll see you in the morning."

E pulls off and Du walks to his house. As he walks up the steps to his room he feels so dizzy. He feels like he's going to pass out. He doesn't want his father to see him high. He will definitely kill him.

He successfully makes it to his room, where he falls asleep.

CHAPTER 3

Du wakes up two hours later. He finally realizes that he doesn't have a clue how he's going to move the pound of weed E gave him. He doesn't have any clientele. Everything he told E's connect was just a front so he would put him on board.

Du begins to make phone calls to let all his friends know what he has. He hopes they'll spread the word.

Three days later he sells one-dime bag. Three more days pass and he still hasn't made another sale.

On the seventh day around 11:00 a.m. the phone rings. Du's father answers, **"As Salaamu Alaikum!"** *(They're Muslims.)*

"Yes, Mr. Muhammad can I speak to Dawud please?" *Dawud is Du's real name.*

"Ibn! Telephone!"

"Hello," says Du.

"Du what's up? How's shit going? Are you finished yet?"

"Are you finished yet?" Du answers defensively.

"Don't tell me you still sitting on that one punk ass pound," E says jokingly.

"Motherfucker, I been finished! I was waiting for you to call me," Du says. *He's lying through his teeth.*

"Alright then, I'm about to come over, and get the money so we can flip again."

"No, not yet, my pops here and he's making me go to the Masjid with him. I'll be back around 8: 30 tonight."

"Alright bet," E replies. **"I'll call you later."**

"Cool!" says Du. *He hangs up. He can't believe he just lied to E like that. He knows it's wrong to lie, but he doesn't want E to* *think he can't move the weed. He only lied because he was scared E wouldn't look out for him the next time.*

"Damn I told him 8:30; now what the fuck am I going to do?" Du asks himself out loud. *He pauses for two minutes and then blurts out* "Casey, let me call Casey."

Casey is a friend of his that E doesn't know. There's no way E will find out.

He beeps Casey and Casey calls him right back.

"What up, Du?"

'Not too much. How about you?"

"Nothing much. What's happening?" Casey asks.

"I was wondering, are you still doing that weed thing?"

"Hell yeah!" Casey screams. "Why, what's up?"

"I got something for you," Du states. "My sister fucks around with this big time nigga. He strong as hell. All he sells is pounds. He hit me with a few. You need to come check it out."

"How much?"

"$800 a pound."

"Eight? Damn, that's good. I'm paying $950 a pound right now. I'm coming right over. If it's good I want three pounds."

Three, got damn, Du thinks to himself. "I only got one pound left. I've been moving them shits all week long, killing them. Not on the block, all wholesale, ounces and quarters. I meant to call you when I first got my package, but niggas won't let me sleep. They call me all day and all night; I need a pound, I need two pounds, you know how shit is."

"Yeah I know," he agrees. "I wish I would've known. Hold that pound for me. I'll be right there."

Ten minutes later the bell rings. Du answers it. It's Casey. They shake hands and hug. "What up, Du?" screams Casey. "I didn't know you were selling wholesale. How long have you been doing that?

"I've been doing that for a minute now," Du lies. But

on the down low, real quiet. **Here it is.** *Du hands him the weed. Casey lifts it up to his nose and takes a sniff.*

"Yeah! This is that good shit," Casey admits. "Here's the money. You did say eight hundred, right?"

"Yeah. I've been hitting motherfuckers at nine hundred, but you my man so you can get it for eight. Don't tell nobody though."

"I know, I know, on the down low," says Casey. "So when are you going to have some more?"

"We got another shipment coming in tonight. I should have my package by tomorrow afternoon."

"Yo, beep me as soon as you get it. I can do about three pounds a week on my block. Let's get this money!"

"Alright, I'll hit you about 2 o'clock."

"Alright, I'll see you tomorrow then!" shouts Casey.

As Du watches him leave, he feels terrible. He can't believe how hard he just fronted to his boy, like he was a drug lord or something. He acted as if he had been selling pound after pound, knowing he only sold one bag all week. He feels guilty but it's too late now. It's done. The only problem is, he didn't make any profit off the deal. That's fine with him. He's just glad that it's gone and E doesn't have a clue of how he moved it. He'll worry about profit when they get the next package. Now that he has hooked up with Casey, he will tell E to get more the next time.

As the weeks fly by they get more and more weed. Du takes his right to Casey without making an extra dime. E never knew.

When they finally got up to ten pounds, the connect gave them a better price. He decreased the price to $700 a pound. Now Du makes $100 profit off of every pound Casey buys.

Before Du realized it, he was on board.

CHAPTER 4

Two months later

"Mr. Johnson, if there isn't anything else to do, I'll punch out now. My bus comes in another ten minutes," says Tony.

"No problem Tony. You're done. I can handle the rest, go ahead and punch out. Enjoy the rest of your weekend," Mr. Johnson replies.

"You too," says Tony.

He punches out and walks to the corner bus stop. Seconds later the bus pulls up. He gets on and grabs a seat in the back.

It's 1:00 p.m. Saturday. I have the whole weekend off, Tony thinks to himself. Although there isn't much he can do. He doesn't have any money. He doesn't get paid until the following Saturday.

It's a long, hot, funky ride. The 5 Kinney bus route is so long. It feels like the driver is taking you for a tour around the world, but Tony appreciates the long ride because it gives him time to think. Tony has been riding for over an hour. Right now he's caught up in deep thought. Tony spends most of his time worrying. His primary concern is being successful.

"Oh shit, next stop!" shouts Tony. "Bus driver, right here! Right here!" he screams, *as they approach South Tenth Street. He almost missed his stop.*

As he steps off the bus, he waves at the barbers in Younger's Barbershop. They're packed as usual. On a Saturday you have to get in there by at least 6:30, in order to get out by noon.

As he walks a little further he hears music approaching. At first he can't make out the words of the song, but as it gets closer it becomes clearer. The hook goes like this. ***HOWEVER DO YOU WANT ME, HOWEVER DO YOU NEED ME.*** *The song just*

18

dropped recently. It's by a group called Soul To Soul. The music is so clear that it sounds like you're in Club Sensations. He still can't see the car yet.

After a couple more steps he finally sees the car coming up the block full speed. The system is so loud you have to cover your ears.

The car is slowing down now. It's a canary yellow Mazda RX7. The interior is piped out yellow and white. He still can't recognize the driver until the car comes to a complete stop, and the driver yells out, **"Ronald McDonald. Ronald motherfucking McDonald, what's up?"** *Now he recognizes who it is. It's E Boogie and Du Drop.*

"What up, ya'll?"

"Man it's 100 motherfucking degrees, and you out here in that tight ass burger suit! You gotta be crazy!" says E.

"Chill E, ease up on him," Du whispers. "Tony where are you headed?"

"Home."

"Get the fuck in Ronald McDonald," says E.

"Chill out with the Ronald McDonald shit. You're starting to piss me off."

"Alright, alright, I'm only bugging," E claims.

For the first time the teasing is really getting on Tony's nerves. He's almost ready to fight E. Tony knows E can't beat him. E is nothing but a punk with a lot of mouth. Tony has a quick temper and everybody knows just how far to go with him before he gets serious and wants to fight.

"Whose car is this?" Tony asks.

"Who driving, motherfucker?" E replies sarcastically, *as he pulls off.* **"I got it selling that garbage ass weed, as you called it. It can't be that bad, I'm riding while you still on the 5 Kinney."**

Tony ignores E's smart remark. **"What year is this?"**

"It's an 86. Do you like it?"

"Like it, I love it," says Tony. I know you getting a lot of

19

pussy with this motherfucker."

"I'm tired of fucking. I been fucking ever since I got this car," E brags.

"Du, what's been up with you?" Tony asks.

"Nothing much; same shit, different day."

"Nigga stop lying to that boy! Tell him the truth, we getting paid!" E interrupts.

"Yeah?" Tony questions.

"Hell yeah," E replies.

"Right here!" Tony blurts out, *as they pass his house.* "Where are you going? You passed by my house."

"We're going downtown," says Du.

"Chill, I still got my uniform on," states Tony. "Let me go to my house and change."

"Hell no motherfucker, don't be ashamed now," E teases.

"Ashamed? I ain't ashamed of shit. I just don't want to be walking around downtown like this."

"You all right," says Du. *By this time it's already too late. They're almost there.*

They park on Branford Place, and get out. E pulls out his Benzi box. He doesn't want anyone to bust his window and steal his radio.

Tony stands there for a second in admiration. The car is such a pretty sight. He even has his name written on the headrests. The whole interior is canary yellow and white, except for the oak wood. He has little pictures of his self posted up on the dashboard. He has so much air freshener in the car; it smells like you're riding in a big watermelon. He has watermelon air freshener trees everywhere. To top it all off, he has chrome rims. They're called Hammers. They cost three thousand for a set.

E jumps out looking like a million bucks. He's wearing yellow and white to match his car. He has on a yellow and white striped Polo rugby, white Polo shorts, yellow and white Polo sun visor, and the new Charles Barkley's. They're white with yellow trimming.

The way they're walking around downtown you would think they're rich, especially E, fronting with that big cellular phone, talking real loud. He's been on the phone the whole time.

Du and E are total opposites. Du is quiet and not as flashy. Du doesn't have to talk loud to get attention. His big gold rope and matching bracelet speaks for itself.

For the first time Tony feels a little embarrassed with his uniform on, but he doesn't let them know it.

As they're walking into the store they're skimming and browsing, while Tony just follows way behind.

The salesman walks over to them. "May I help you?"

"Yeah!" E shouts. "I need three pairs of Adidas forums, three pairs of Guess jeans, and three Champion t- shirts. My size is 10 in the sneakers, 32 jeans, and extra large in the t-shirt. They'll give you their sizes."

"E, I ain't got no money," Tony whispers.

"You don't need money. You're with us," E explains. "Now give the man your size."

"I'm alright, E," Tony says reluctantly.

"Tell the man your size," says Du. "Later for that modest shit, we family."

"Size 8 shoe, 31 jeans, and extra large shirt," Tony finally says. "Good looking out, E."

"Don't worry about it schoolboy. Just keep doing what you doing, and we're going to keep doing what we doing. In ten years we're going to need your brains to run our businesses.

The salesman piles everything on the counter, and the clerk rings it all up. "That will be $640 please," she says.

"Make it $700 even; get yourself a pair of Reebok aerobics on me, alright baby?" E asks the beautiful red bone girl.

"Thank you," she replies. *She's blushing from ear to ear.*

"Write your number down on this receipt," E says confidently, *as he passes the receipt back to her.*

She writes the number down and hands the paper back to

him. "Here you go sweetie. What's your number?" she asks, *while she stands there holding the pen on the paper, getting ready to write his number down.*

"1-800-getting money!" E yells out. "Ask for E Boogie," he says, *as he laughs in her face.* "Syke, I'm only bugging. What time do you get off?"

"At 5," she replies.

"I'll pick you up at 5:01. I'll be in the front. My car is canary yellow. You'll see me."

"5:01?"

"5:01!" he shouts, *as they're walking out of the store.*

"Yo E, she look good as hell," says Tony. "Did you see all that pretty hair?"

"Fuck the hair; did you see that fat ass?" E asks. "All that ass she got, and you in there looking at her hair. Du what the fuck is wrong with this guy?"

Du laughs. "He'll be alright."

"I'm going to fuck the shit out of that bitch tonight," Du claims.

"I bet you, you don't fuck her," says Du.

"How much do you want to bet?" E asks.

"$500, I bet you don't fuck her tonight!" Du challenges.

"You right," E agrees. "I'm not going to fuck her tonight; it won't even be nighttime yet. I'm picking her up at 5:01. I'll be fucking her by 5:25," he says with confidence.

"Yeah right!"

"No bullshit!"

"Yo E, thanks again for the gear," says Tony.

"Will you shut the fuck up with that thank you shit? I told you we family."

For the duration of the ride, they all sit quietly listening to the music. After about an hour and a half of riding Du tells E to drop him and Tony off at Tony's house. Du decides to hang out with Tony being that they haven't seen each other for almost three months.

As they approach the house, E turns the music down and say's, "**Alright ya'll.**"

"**Later!**" screams Du.

"**Yo E, leave my clothes in the trunk. I can't take that shit in the house; my mother knows I didn't get paid this week,**" says Tony.

"**You a funny motherfucker,**" E jokes. "**What are we going to do with you?**"

As E pulls off he yells out the window, "**At 5:20 I'm going to call the house. I'm going to let her ask for you while my dick is up in her.**"

"**Yeah whatever,**" Du replies.

The two go up to Tony's room and start up the video game as usual.

"**Damn ya'll getting paid,**" Tony blurts out.

"**Little something, something,**" Du replies.

"**Why didn't you buy a car yet?**"

"**My car is in the shop getting painted.**"

"**What kind of car?**"

"**I got a Honda CRX. They're painting it orange and piping my seats out orange and white.**"

"**You got rims?**" Tony asks. "**What you got, those hammers like E?**"

"**Nah, I got Auto forms,**" Du replies. "**Later for that shit, what's up with you?**"

"**Oh I didn't tell you, I'm leaving the end of the month. I got accepted to Virginia State.**"

"**That's alright! "I know your mother is proud as hell, her boy going off to college. How are you paying for it?**"

"**My father told me not to worry about it. He said he'd pay for it. I guess he's trying to make up for not doing shit for me all my life.**"

"**Hey fuck it, now is the time you really need him and if he's going to be there then that's cool.**" *The boys continue to play the game.*

23

Meanwhile E is home getting ready for his date.
"What the fuck am I going to put on?" *E blurts out, talking to his self.*

He begins looking through his closet. He reaches for his yellow velour Pierre Cardin sweat suit. He puts that on with his white Reebok classics and a yellow headband. He looks in the mirror posing from every view. **"Yeah!"** **he blurts out,** *while bopping his head. He then looks at the clock and runs out the door.*

CHAPTER 5

"What's up, baby?" E asks.

"You sweetie, you're late," the clerk replies.

"Five minutes? I know you're not going to deduct me for that."

"I sure am. Your car really smells good."

"You never did tell me your name," says E.

"Aisha, and what is your real name?"

"E Boogie."

"No, the name your mother gave you. You look like an Ernest or an Eric."

"Chill baby, my name is E Boogie. So you always get in cars with strangers?"

"Hold up, now you're starting to scare me, asking questions like that."

"Easy baby, I won't hurt you unless you ask me to. So where is your boyfriend?"

"I don't have one."

"What, ya'll broke up?"

"No, I never had one."

"Yeah… alright. How old are you?"

"Eighteen," Aisha replies. "Niggas are the last thing on my mind. I mean, I have hung out with a few guys and kicked it on the phone but no commitment. I'm just concentrating on work and school. I want to do something with my life."

Uh oh, no commitment she must be a hottie. E thinks to him self. He knows for sure this one will be easy. It will be like taking candy from a baby.

As they're riding, Aisha sits quietly. She just sits there

*dazing off into space, while E drives around the whole town, hitting
all the hot spots, blowing the horn and yelling to damn near every
one on every block.*

"**Where are we going?**" **Aisha asks.**

"**Just sit back and cool out,**" **E replies.**

*They drive for another twenty minutes before pulling up to
Livingston Mall.*

"**Come on, I want to pick up a few things,**" **says E.**

*As they walk to the Mall, E can't help but notice how
everyone turns their heads to watch Aisha. At times, E has to take
double looks at her. He has dozens of girls, but he has to admit
she's in the top five. She has everything, pretty face, long hair, fat
ass and big tits. All he envisions is her stretched out naked.*

"**Hello…. I'm talking to you, what are you thinking
about?**"

"**You,**" **E mischievously answers.**"

"**What about me?**"

"**I was thinking how good you're going to look walking
down the aisle.**"

"**Nigga please…. Enough with the games.**"

"**Hold up right here, let's go in here,**" **E suggests.**

*They walk into the eyeglass store. E skims around through
the cases on the wall, before finally locating what he wants.* "**Can I
get these frames over here?**"

"**Which ones?**" **the salesman asks.**

"**The Polo frames right here,**" **E points out.** *E tries them
on and turns to Aisha.* "**These me?**

"**Yeah they you, they make you look intelligent;
intelligent hoodlum. Huh, huh, huh,**" **she laughs.**

"**Let me get these,**" **E says to the salesman.**

"**Don't you want to know the price?**" **the salesman asks.**

"**Money doesn't matter!**" **says E,** *as he pulls stacks of
money from every pocket.*

"**Okay, sir that will be $320.**"

E pays the man, and from there they head down to Macy's,

straight to the women's dept.

Now, E is skimming over women shoes. He picks up a sneaker and asks, **"Aisha what size do you wear?"**

"Size six."

"Give me a six and I need a pocket book to match. Fuck it throw in the shades too," E says arrogantly.

As she tries on the sneakers and walks around the store she asks, **"What are these?"**

"What are they? Mark Cross, you never heard of that?"

"No!"

"Baby, you got a lot to learn and I'm just the nigga to teach you. Yo, salesman what's the total on that?"

"The bag $550, the sneakers $220 and the shades $160, that will be $930.

"Bag it up!"

"Thank you sir, and have a nice day," says the salesman.

"I have a nice day everyday," E replies sarcastically, *as they exit the store and walk back to the car.*

E takes route 78 to Parkway South. From there he jumps on Route 22 and pulls up in front of Red Lobster. **"Are you hungry?"** he asks.

"I'm starving," she replies.

"Your name and starving will never be mentioned in the same sentence ever again. You got the right motherfucker now."

"You're crazy!" Aisha shouts.

"Yeah crazy for you," E replies.

"Uh boy, more game."

The waitress walks toward them. **"How many?"**

"Two," E replies.

"Name?" the waitress asks.

"Mr. and Mrs. E Boogie."

"That'll be a ten-minute wait."

As they sit in the lobby waiting to get seated, E's cellular phone starts ringing. **"Yeah?"** E answers.

"Yo, you got my $500 nigga?" screams the voice on the other end.

"Hello!" E yells.

"What's up motherfucker? Where you at? Why didn't you call us yet?" the voice screams out again. "It's Du, motherfucker!"

E walks toward the bathroom so he can talk privately. "What's up?" he asks.

"Nigga, are you fucking yet?"

"Nah, not yet, I'm just setting her up. This shit is going to be so easy, trust me. After I fuck her I'm coming to your house so you can smell my dick, alright?" he asks, *laughing as he speaks.*

"Where the fuck ya'll at?" Du asks.

"Route 22, Red Lobster, she wanted to fuck me in the car, but I wasn't ready to fuck her yet." *E is lying through his teeth.* "I wanted to feed her before I fuck her brains out. Being that this will be her last time seeing me, the least I could do is give her a meal. You know how I do, love em, and leave em."

"Mr. and Mrs. E Boogie!" screams the voice over the loud speaker.

"Du, they just called my name to be seated. Later."
E hangs the phone up, and hurries to the lobby where Aisha is standing.

As they're walking through the restaurant E grabs hold of her hand, and begins pimping extra hard as he's walking. He stares in the faces of every male that looks at her.

After being seated, they eat and talk for almost two hours. After they finish eating, they exit the building and walk back to the car.

Before E pulls off he decides to test her out. He leans over for a kiss. To his surprise she sticks her entire tongue in his mouth.

"Was that dessert?" *E asks. Aisha doesn't answer. She just smiles. As he puts the car in drive he grabs his rock hard dick, and thinks to himself, I am going to tear that pussy up. He then puts an old Blue Magic slow tape in the radio and pulls off. The song "Sideshow" blares through the speakers. The sound system makes them feel as if they're at a live concert.*

As he's driving, he tries to figure out how he's going to crack for the sex. He finally speaks. **"It's not past your curfew is it? I don't want to get you in trouble."**

"Trouble, curfew, you're talking stupid. I'm grown!" *That is exactly what E wanted to hear.*

"How grown?" **E asks.**

"Grown enough, motherfucker!"

"Seriously, how long can you stay out?" **he asks,** *still gaming on her.*

"Until I'm ready to go in," **she answers.**

"Well what time do you want to go in?"

"I'll let you know when," **she replies.**

"How about I keep you with me, and never take you home?" **he asks,** *just kidding with her.*

"You wouldn't do that."

"You know what? That's what I'm going to do. You're staying with me."

"Staying with you where?" **she asks.**

"Does it matter? As long as we are together that's what counts, right?" *Aisha doesn't respond she just lays back in the seat, enjoying the music.*

They're now riding on Routes 1 and 9 South. They pull up to the Loop Motel. Before turning into the parking lot, E waits for Aisha's response. He wants to see if she's going to refuse, but she doesn't. She just sits there with her eyes closed as if she's sleeping.

After he checks in and gets the key, they both enter the room skeptically. E enters the room like that as a part of his game. Aisha on the other hand is nervous because she has never been there before. She doesn't know what to expect.

The room is big and beautiful. Inside the room there is a Jacuzzi, a fireplace, and a heart shaped bed.

"What's up baby, why are you so quiet? Loosen up."

"Shut up," she replies. "Is this where you take all your bitches?"

"All what bitches? I don't have any bitches!" he lies. "Have you ever been in a Jacuzzi?"

"Nope," she answers quickly.

"C'mon let's get in."

He prepares the water. After he pours the bubble bath in, he strips down to his Calvin Klein boxers. Aisha looks him up and down. She didn't imagine him having such a nice body. He's slim framed, yet and still he's so muscular.

"Go ahead take off your clothes," E suggests.

Aisha's heart is pounding hard. She begins to take off her sandals first. Then slowly she opens her pants. As she unzips her zipper you can see her fine pubic hair curled up over her panty line. She slowly slides her pants down.

That's a fat pussy, he thinks to himself, as he swallows the lump that formed in his throat.

She takes off her blouse. Her tiny bra can't hold her big tits. They're hanging out everywhere. Bare skin peeks from every angle. They're so round and firm. Her hard nipples are poking through her bra.

There she stands with a white cotton bra on and panties to match. As she turns to put her clothes on the chair, E sneaks a peek at her ass. One whole side of her panties is wedged in the crack of her ass, leaving her left cheek fully exposed. As she turns back around, she slowly pulls her panties out of her round ass. "Well? What are you staring at?" she asks, *as she stands there looking embarrassed.* "You get in first," she insists.

"Go ahead, you get in first," he demands. *He's trying to stall her. He can't get up yet because his dick is so hard from all the excitement of watching her undress.* "Turn the lights off," he says, *still trying to stall her.*

As she goes over to turn off the lights, E hurries into the Jacuzzi.

They must have been kissing and rubbing in the Jacuzzi for two hours before E finally says, **"This water is starting to get cold. I'm getting out."**

They both stand there drying off. Goose bumps cover Aisha's naked body. After completely drying off, she wiggles into her tightly fitted panties, and she plops onto the bed, landing on her stomach. Before E is fully dried off, he jumps in the bed behind her.

He starts massaging her feet, and then he licks her toes, one by one. Aisha is so tense, but as he slowly rubs her calves, he feels her begin to loosen up. He begins kissing her on her legs; all the way up from her ankles to her calves. He slowly licks up and down her thighs. When he gets to the top of her thigh he continues to lick until he reaches her back, where he plants little kisses all over. He slowly drags his tongue up her spine until he gets to her neck. He starts licking her ear, and then he turns her head to him and licks her lips around and around teasing her tongue with his. Once again he kisses her back and begins licking all the way back down to her butt, where he plants soft kisses. He then spreads her legs wide open and begins licking and kissing her inner thigh. E has already pre ejaculated. His underwear is sticking to the head of his dick. He now decides to make his move. He slides her panties to the side and slowly slides his finger into her tight pussy. She's so tight he has to force his finger in. It's so wet and slippery inside. He fingers her, as she lays there moaning and breathing hard. He gently strokes her button. She begins to squirm and pump as if she's fucking his finger. E is convinced. She's ready now. Finally he turns her over and slides her panties down to her knees. **"E stop,"** she whispers, *while still breathing heavy.*

"Stop, what do you mean stop?"

"Please stop," she begs. **"Not now please."** *She's now pulling her panties back up.* **"We don't even know each other. I don't even know your real name,"** she sighs. **"Is that why you spent all that money on me, you were trying to buy my pussy!"** *She's starting to yell and get excited.*

"Calm down," he begs.

"No! You thought I would fuck you for a pocketbook

and some motherfucking lobster? Do you do this to all your
bitches? Take me home you dirty dick nigga!" she screams.
"And take your shit back, give it to whatever bitch you meet
tomorrow, save yourself some money!" *She begins to cry.* "Take
me home!" she yells, *as she puts her clothes on. E quickly gets
dressed and they jump in the car.*

*Aisha has been sniffling, and crying the whole ride. He
doesn't know what to say. This has never happened to him before.
He has pulled this same stunt a hundred times and it never failed
him until now.*

As they approach Chadwick Avenue, Aisha screams, "**Drop
me off right here!**"

"I'm sorry," E pleads. "Here take your stuff."

"I don't want that shit; shove it up your ass!" she yells *as
she slams the door.*

*E pulls off slow, like 5 miles an hour. He's shocked at the
way she performed.*

*He drives around for the rest of the night replaying the
situation in his head over and over again, until he finally goes home
and falls asleep.*

CHAPTER 6

The next morning E wakes up around 8:00 a.m. Before he even wipes the sleep out of his eyes he starts fumbling through his pockets, looking for Aisha's phone number.

"I got it!" he blurts out loud. *He starts dialing the number and the phone begins to ring. After three rings someone finally picks up.*

"Hello," whispers the voice, *sounding half sleep.*

"Hello can I speak to Ai," *Click. The phone hangs up before he can finish asking for her. E thinks someone may have accidentally hung the phone up, so he decides to call back.*

"Hello?" answers the voice.

"Hello," E replies. *CLICK he gets the dial tone again. After pausing for a moment, standing there staring at the phone in his hand, he finally hangs up. Fuck it; I'll go by her job later, he thinks to himself, as he walks to the bathroom to shower.*

Now he's dressed and ready to walk out the door. As he passes the mirror he stops and stares at himself. He looks fresh but for some strange reason he feels terrible.

E is on his way to pick Du up. If it weren't for the business they had to handle, he wouldn't even go. He's not in a big rush to see Du because of the bet they made about Aisha. If Du finds out what happened, he'll be sure to clown E.

BEEP, bEEP, bEEP, bEEP. "Du!" E screams, *from the car window*

"Here I come," Du replies, *as he walks down the steps. E has to admit Du is definitely looking fresh today. He's wearing a royal blue, velour Fila sweat suit with the headband to match, and bone white Fila sneakers.*

"So what happened? Did you fuck her or what?" Du **asks,** *before he even gets all the way in the car.*

"Nah, I didn't fuck her," E answers hesitantly.

"I told you motherfucker! Give me my money!"

"No, it wasn't like that. I didn't want to fuck her. She was all over me but I just didn't want her. She begged and begged. She was like, E please fuck me. What's wrong with me, why don't you want me? I mean, once I got her in the car and took a close up of her, she wasn't all that. Actually she looks funny as hell. I didn't even want the pussy. We just ate and I dropped her off. I think all that begging turned me off."

"Nigga, later for that bullshit you're talking, just give me my $500."

"Alright motherfucker I got you," E claims. "Did you bring the weed money?"

"Yeah, here it is right here, $3,500," Du replies, *as he hands the money over.*

"Alright, we'll meet with him after I go back home and get my money."

They proceed to E's house. E is dying to call Aisha but he can't because he doesn't want Du to find out what really happened.

As they're pulling in front of the house, Du lays his seat all the way back, and says, "I'll squat for you in here."

Good, E thinks to himself. Now he can call Aisha again.

As he walks up the steps he starts dialing Aisha's job number.

"Dr. Jays!" shouts the voice on the phone.

"Hello, can I speak to Aisha?"

"May I ask who is calling?"

"Tell her E, she'll know who it is."

"Ok, please hold."

The phone goes dead for a few seconds, before he hears the voice speak again.

"Hello?"

"Yeah," E replies.

"Aisha isn't accepting any calls from you, sorry."

"What?" E asks. *CLICK, they hang up on him.*

When he finally reaches his room, he goes straight to his closet. He grabs his Timberland box from the top shelf. He opens the box and counts the money just to make sure it's all there. He counts once and then he counts it again.

"Hold the fuck up!" he shouts. "Somebody has been fucking with my money! Ma!"

He looks over the entire house for her. Finally he finds her in the basement. When he busts through the door, she's sitting in the corner all huddled over, as if she's trying to hide. All she has on is a bra and some shorts. Her hair is wild and her eyes are stretched wide open. When she spots him she immediately hides something behind her back.

"Ma, what the fuck are you doing down here? Have you been in my room?"

"What, your room?"

"Mom what do you have behind your back?"

E runs over and grabs her. They wrestle until they hit the floor. She has something in her fist. He tries to pry her hand open but it's almost impossible because of the way she's kicking and screaming. She even tries to scratch his eyes with her free hand. Finally he gets her hand open. What he sees makes him furious. It's a crack pipe. He lifts her up by her arm and slams her back to the floor, causing her to drop her pipe.

"You fucking crack head!" he screams. "You smoked my motherfucking money up!"

"So what, you drug dealing bastard! If you don't want me to take it, don't bring it in my motherfucking house. If you leave some more I'll smoke that up too! I told you not to bring that street shit in my house!"

E can't do a thing. Regardless of what, she's still his mother. He stands there looking at her, as the tears slowly creep down his face. Mom picks her pipe up from the floor and sprints up the stairs.

E doesn't know what he's going to tell his man. He's $2,000 short. He can't believe it. She smoked up $2000. E tries to get his self together before he gets back into the car but Du notices the tears in his eyes.

"**What's the matter, are you alright?**"

E hesitates before he answers. "**Nope, I'm fucked up, my moms back smoking that shit again. She stole 2000 out my stash.**" *The tears start to roll down his face all over again.* "**I just caught her in the basement with the pipe in her hand.**

"**Damn, I thought she chilled.**"

"**She did, it's that crack head ass nigga she be fucking with. Every time she gets her self together, he finds a way to get her back hooked. I think he's scared she might leave him if she gets her life together,**" **says E.**

"**Damn she smoked up $2000?**"

"**Yeah, I heard them running in and out all last night and early this morning but I didn't know they were spending my dough,**" **E explains.** "**Now my part of the money is short. My man wants his money. What the fuck am I going to tell him?**"

"**Word up,**" **Du agrees.**

"**I'm supposed to meet this cat in ten minutes. Got damn it!**"

On their way to the meeting place, E thinks of all kinds of stories to tell his man. He's too embarrassed to tell him, his mother is a crack head and she smoked the money up.

When they turn onto Avon Avenue they don't see the convertible Saab he normally drives. In the space where he normally parks, there sits a black, two door 300 CE, Mercedes Benz.

As they get closer to the car E's man sticks his hand out the window.

"**There he goes,**" **says E.** *E is disappointed. He was hoping his man wasn't there yet. That would have given him more time to come up with a better story.* "**I'm going over and talk to him, you just squat right here.**"

E walks over to the car and hops in the backseat as usual.

"What's up Boogie Baby?"

"Nothing much," E replies. "Yo, the money is a little short, I ran into a problem," E whispers.

"Short, what do you mean short? How short are you?"

"$2,000 short," E mumbles.

"I know you didn't say 2 grand! That's more than short, you trying to play me the fuck out!"

"I'm not trying to play you. I'll pay you back off this one."

"What the fuck happened?" he asks.

He's pissed off. E can hear it in his voice. This is going to be a problem. "I, I, I, got robbed." *That was the only lie E could come up with.*

"Where were you when you got robbed?"

"On, on the block," E stutters. Slap! *Before E could spit the words from his mouth, his man had already slapped the shit out of him.*

E sits there holding his lip. The corner of his mouth is bleeding. E can't believe it. He just got bitch slapped.

"Yo, I'll get that money back to you. I swear to God I'm not trying out play you out. I wouldn't do that to you. You haven't showed me nothing but love ever since I met you. Please give me a chance to pay you back," he begs.

E's man turns to the driver, "Yo man, get out and fuck this little nigga up!"

The driver gets out of the car and attempts to drag E out. E is squirming like a fish. He's holding on for dear life. He damn near snatches the headrest off, trying to keep him from pulling him out the car.

After he finally pulls E from the car, he picks him up and earth slams him face first onto the concrete.

"I got you, I got you!" E pleads.

"I know you got me!"

Du takes notice to what's happening and he runs over to

rescue E.

"What the fuck are you running over here for? You better stay in a child's place!" *The driver is now stomping E and kicking him in the face.*

Du runs over to the driver and tries to push him off of E. By this time E's man already has his gun pointed at Du's chest. **"Little man if you move I'll blow your fucking head off!"** *he shouts.* **"I told you to stay in your place,"** *he says.* **"Chill, let him up!"** *he instructs.*

E manages to stumble onto his feet. His left eye is swollen and his mouth is extremely bloody. **"I told you I would pay you back,"** *says E.* **"Ya'll didn't have to do all that,"** *he says, with a shaky voice.*

"Motherfucker, don't tell me what the fuck we had to do! You ain't have to spend my motherfucking money either! How are you two motherfuckers going to get my money back to me?"

"It wasn't him. He had his part of the money," E explains. **"If you give me another chance, I promise I'll pay you back a couple hundred at a time."**

"I know what happened, you spent my money on your little bitches, that's what happened, you dumb ass nigga."

E doesn't reply. He would rather let him think that, than to let him know his mother is a crack head.

"I know what I'm going to do, give me your car keys!" *he shouts. E slowly passes the keys to him.* **"I'm going to take your little raggedy ass car for collateral. When I get my dough, you can have your car back."**

E doesn't like the sound of that, but he's afraid to speak up.

He then passes E the weed. **"Here's the work, hit me as soon as you finish."** *He jumps in the Benz while the other guy squeezes into E's little tight ass car. They pull off, leaving E and Du standing on the curb.*

E hasn't said a word since they pulled off. Watching them pull off in his car, while they have to walk home really made him feel like a sucker. He had been totally disrespected. He really felt bad because Du was there to see him get violated like that. The bad part was he didn't even try to fight back.

"I wish I had a gun. I would have popped him," says Du. "He can't fight. That's why he so quick to pull out that gun all the time. I know I could whip his ass, he straight pussy."

"I didn't want you to get involved, that was my problem," E claims.

"I had to get involved your problem is my problem; we're together in this."

Meanwhile today is Tony's last day working at the burger joint.

"Mr. Johnson, I'm punching out, if that is okay with you?"

"Sure Tony! Here's your last check. I just want to tell you how proud I am of you going away to college. I wish you all the luck in the world. I can see you will be very successful in life, if you keep your head on right. Go to school get your education and everything else will fall in place. Always remember; trouble is easy to get into but hard to get out of."

"I know Mr. J; I don't have any plans of getting into any trouble. I'm just trying to do the right thing." *Mr. Johnson embraces Tony for the last time and Tony runs out to catch the bus that's on its way up the block.*

As Tony approaches the block he notices that E and Du are not out there, so he doesn't bother to get off. That's even better, because he has packing to do. He's leaving for College in two weeks.

As the weeks flew by Tony hadn't seen E or Du. Everybody was sort of doing their own thing. Tony was busy, packing and getting his paper work in order and E and Du were trying to pay off their debt.

Every now and then E would call Aisha but never did she

39

answer. He didn't have time to go down to her job because he played the block all day. Anyway, he didn't have his car and he couldn't walk down there, she might think he was off board.

CHAPTER 7

Ring, ring, ring! Tony reaches for the phone as he looks over at the clock. It's 2 in the morning.

Who the fuck is calling at two in the morning? He asks himself. "Hello?" **he answers,** *with a groggy voice.*

"Who is this?" **the caller questions.**

"Hello!" **Tony yells.**

"Is this Tony?" **the caller asks.**

"Who is this? Dad?" *Tony recognizes the voice of his father.*

"Yeah, this is your father."

"What's up Pop? Is everything all right? What's the matter, it's two in the morning?"

"I don't give a fuck what time it is," **his father slurs.**

"Dad, are you alright? Have you been drinking?"

"Hell yeah, I've been drinking. You are a piece of shit! You're a punk, faggot ass, piece of shit. Do you know that?"

"Pop, what are you talking about?" *Tony now realizes that his father is drunk out of his mind.*

"What the fuck do you mean, what the fuck am I talking about? You ain't going to be nothing but a punk ass faggot!"

"Dad, call me tomorrow when you sober up."

"Fuck you Tony! Do you hear me? Fuck you! Fuck you and your bitch ass mother! Tony I will fuck you up, the same way I used to fuck your mother up!"

Now Tony is enraged, remembering how he grew up watching his father beat his mother. The thought of it made him hate his father all over again. He promised himself he would repay his father one day but over the years he sort of put it in the back

41

of his mind. Now that his father is bragging about it, the fire is rekindling. It's sort of like opening an old wound.

"Dad, I'm hanging up, you're drunk."

"Tony, do you think you can fuck me up? Huh, you faggot ass nigga?"

"Dad, what are you talking about? You're drunk, just call me tomorrow."

"Tony, fuck you, fuck your mother and fuck that college! I'm not paying for shit. You want to go to college? You and your bitch ass mother will have to pay for it. I'm not paying for shit. I mean that shit, Tony! Bye, you punk ass, piece of shit ass faggot!" Click.

Before Tony could respond, his father hung up on him. Tony can't believe what just happened. His father had let him down all of his life but never like this. He thought his father paying for college was his way of making up for all the disappointments and lies. What will he tell people when they ask him, why hasn't he left for college yet? What will he tell his mom? He can't tell his mom. She can barely pay the bills as it is. He doesn't want to pressure her like that.

All that night Tony tossed and turned until he finally cried himself to sleep. He doesn't know what to he's going to do.

CHAPTER 8

E and Du finally paid off their debt. E was so happy to get his car back. Du finally got his car out of the shop. Everything is back in order, business as usual.

It's a beautiful day downtown Newark. It's the first of the month, so it's very crowded.

E and Du are sitting parked in front of Dr. Jay's. E is sitting in his car and Du is sitting parked right behind him. E has the canary yellow Mazda RX 7 and Du has the orange Honda CRX.

Du gets out and walks up to E's car.

"Do you want me to go in there and see if she's there?" **Du asks.**

"Nah, let's just squat out here, she's about to get off soon."

"Here she comes!" **Du shouts.**

"Watch out, let me out!"

E runs over to the doorway where Aisha is standing.

"What's up Aisha, long time no hear from?

Aisha stands there looking in the opposite direction as if E isn't there.

"Look, I apologize for that night. I really like you. These past weeks have been driving me crazy, not being able to contact you. What can I do to prove to you that I really want to be with you? I'll cut all my female friends off in front of you. It will just be you and me." *She still isn't responding.*

"Move, my ride is here!" *She steps toward the curb. Seconds later a white 535 BMW with tinted windows pulls up. She gets in and they pull off.*

E stands there feeling stupid. He's so embarrassed.

*A couple of boys on the corner laugh at him as he jumps
back in his car. Du pulls side by side with him.*

"Follow me, Tony just beeped me. I'm going to his
house."

*After they get to Tony's house and park they don't go right
in. They stand in the middle of the street and talk.*

"Who was that she got in the car with?" Du asks.

"I don't know."

"He must be paid up, that 535 just came out this year.
That shit was fresh as hell."

"You like them? That shit ugly," says E, knowing he's
lying. "Yo, I gotta get her."

"You should have fucked her when she was begging you
to, now she probably in the BM begging him to fuck her." *E
doesn't respond. He forgot that he had lied about that night.*

Tony comes to the door and interrupts the conversation.
"Your shit looks good Du. You're killing Tweety Bird over
there."

"Shut up you broke ass nigga," says E.

"Syke, I'm only bugging, ya'll killing them. Yo Du, what
did your father say about the car?"

"My father doesn't know about this car. Are you crazy,
Big Muslim would kill me." *Big Muslim is the nickname they
gave Du's father. He's 6'6, 280 pounds. He's a big nigga and he
doesn't play. Du is scared to death of him.*

"Where do you park it?" Tony asks.

"I park at E's house."

"E, why are you so quiet?" Tony asks.

"I'm not in the best of moods today," he replies.

"That Aisha bitch is driving him crazy," says Du. "She's
not fucking with him. We went to her job to scoop her up, she
jumped in a 5, left E right on the curb looking stupid."

"Got Damn! You talk too much, just like a bitch."

"Was it white?" Tony asks.

"Yeah," Du replies.

"I know who he is. His name is Cool Breeze," says Tony. "He's from the Vailsburg section. He's paid up."

"How do you know him?" E asks.

"A couple of kids in my school are always talking about him. I think they're his runners. He picks them up from West Side everyday."

"Is he young?" E asks.

"Nah, I think he's like twenty-seven."

"Twenty-seven, fucking with young ass schoolgirls?" E questions.

"Nigga, you're just mad because he's tearing that little pussy up, while you chasing her around!" Du shouts.

As they walk to Du's car E pauses for a moment, thinking to himself how he's going to back up off Aisha. After all, he knows he can't compete with that guy. That's why she wasn't impressed with the expensive gifts. Now he knows why his game plan didn't work.

"Yo Du, I got a problem," Tony admits.

"What's up?" Du asks.

"My father called me at two this morning, drunk, cursing me out. Telling me he isn't paying for my school and how I'm not going to be anything but a fag."

"Yeah, what's up with him? What did your mom say?"

"She doesn't know. I didn't tell her. I don't want to stress her out. She's scared that if I stay here I might turn to the streets. If I tell her this, she's really going to be bugging."

"So what are you going to do?"

"I got to find another job, save my money up and go to school next year, hopefully."

"That's fucked up, Tony. You know I'm here if you need me."

"Yeah I know that," says Tony.

"So are you rolling with us or what?" Du asks.

"Nah, I'm waiting for my mom to get off work now so I can break the news to her."

"Alright, later on then."

"Peace. C'mon E, let's roll out."

45

CHAPTER 9

It didn't take Tony long to find a new job. He's working through a temporary agency. He has been working nights for the past couple of weeks. He works from 12am to 6am.

"Tony, wake up! Break is over," says a co-worker.

Tony cracks his eyes open. He looks at his watch; it's 2am. **"Good looking out. I'm glad you caught me before the supervisor did," says Tony.**

"Where do they have you working tonight?" the co-worker asks.

"On the dock, I'm loading and unloading," Tony replies.

"Are you working with Peterson?"

"Nah, they got me with Flaco tonight," Tony replies.

"Damn, I hate working with that stupid motherfucker. He's lazy as hell. The night seems so long working with him."

"He's alright with me, I don't mind working with him. You just gotta get to know him," Tony claims.

"Fuck that stupid motherfucker!" says the co-worker. "Let me get over here to my post, later."

"Alright later," Tony replies.

As Tony walks back to the dock he notices Flaco is still sleeping. He grabs Flaco by the shoulder and shakes him to wake him. **"Flaco, Flaco, trabajo."** *Flaco sits up.*

Nobody likes to work with Flaco because he can't speak English. Being that he can't understand you there is no way of holding a conversation with him, so that means 8 hours of straight work. Tony learned a little Spanish in high school so Flaco and him are able to hold small conversations. Flaco is the nickname the co-workers gave him. It means skinny, in Spanish.

"Gracias, poppy," says Flaco.

"No problemo," Tony replies. "Mucho trabajo," Tony adds.

"Si verdad," Flaco replies.

After Flaco thanked Tony for waking him, they work in silence for another 2 hours.

Tony breaks the silence with, **"Flaco, cuanto anos tiene?"** (How old are you?)

"Biente y ocho anos," (Twenty-eight years old.)

"Cuantos anos tu vives en New Jersey? (How many years have you lived in New Jersey?)

"Tres anos." (Three years.)

Then to Tony's surprise, Flaco whispers something in English. **"Tony, you can talk to me in English."**

"What did you say?" Tony asks.

"I said, you can talk English to me. I can understand you, Poppy."

"You can? Then how come everybody in here says you can't?"

"Because I told them that," Flaco replies. **"I told them that because I don't want to fuck with them. I come here to work, not talk. I don't need friends. Friends get in your business."**

"Damn, you got the whole job fooled."

"Tony, please don't let any body else know," Flaco begs. **"I like you because you are so different from the rest of these guys here."**

"Can I ask you a question?"

"Sure," Flaco replies.

"When these guys call you all kinds of names in English, you can really understand them, huh?"

"I understand every word they say; stupid motherfucker, Goya bean eating motherfucker, everything poppy," Flaco admits. **"I don't say anything because I don't want to blow my cover, so I just sit there and act like the stupid motherfucker**

they call me."

"So in all reality they're the stupid motherfuckers, huh?"

"Yeah, basically," Flaco answers. *They both laugh.*

"I like you Poppy. I've been checking you out. Never once did you disrespect me and on several occasions I even heard you defend me."

"Nah Flaco, I would never talk bad about you. I'm not like that."

"I know that Poppy. I have something else to tell you but you have to promise me you wont tell anyone. I mean no one at all."

"I swear!"

"You know why I'm working here?"

"Why?" Tony asks.

"I'm on the run," says Flaco.

"I'm on the run from New York."

"Yeah? For what?"

"Poppy, a few months ago I got caught with a lot of cocaine. When I got bailed out I never went back to court, that's why I'm working here. Poppy, I'm not scared of jail but the thing is if I'm convicted I'll go to jail, then they will deport me back to Dominican Republic. I don't ever want to go back there."

"Will they send you back for good?"

"Yeah, for good. That is why I claim to speak no English, so everybody will think I'm a stupid motherfucker and hopefully they won't bother me."

At this moment Tony's whole attitude toward Flaco has changed. Not for better or worse, it just makes him feel good to know Flaco trusts him enough to tell him something as serious as that.

"Poppy, please don't tell nobody."

"Flaco, I will never repeat this to anyone, I promise."

"I'm sure you won't. I know real people when I see

them."

    Meanwhile on the other side of town, E and Du just left Bergenfield's skating rink. That's where everybody goes on Saturday night, and when that's over everybody meets up at White Castle on Elizabeth Avenue.

    "Got damn, it's a lotta bitches out here tonight!" says E, *as Du pulls up in White Castle's parking lot.* **"I should have driven my own car. I know I would have taken something home with me tonight,"** E *says arrogantly.*

    "Yeah right," says Du, *as he parks.*

    E is definitely right, there are girls everywhere. They're sitting along the curb and standing in the middle of the street. They have the streets blocked off as the guys on the motorcycles wheelie and do stunts up and down the street. It's like a car show out there. Any kind of car you could dream of having is out there, BMW's, Benz's, Jaguars, Range Rovers, Milanos, Cadillac Allantes, Mazeratis, everything.

    E and Du walk around kicking it with the people they know, as more and more people pull in.

    It's all fun until some girls start fighting over some dude. After E and Du watch the fight, they walk over to the entrance, where Du spots a white BMW pulling in. **"E, here comes that white BM.**

    "Where, where?"

    "Over there," says Du, *as he points across the parking lot.* **"The door is opening, he's getting out."**

    E's heart is pounding. He's finally going to see what Cool Breeze looks like.

    The door opens and the driver gets out. To his surprise, it is Aisha.

    She's driving that niggas car, E thinks to himself.

    Then shortly after that the passenger door pops open.

    "She's with another girl; I'm about to go over there," says E.

    "Chill, don't play yourself again."

*As E starts to walk over there he peeps someone else
climbing out of the back seat. It's a dude. He's tall and slim.
He's wearing a blue Gucci sweat suit, with some all white Gucci
sneakers, and a fishermen's hat.*

That must be Cool Breeze, E thinks to himself.

*E is too embarrassed to stop because Aisha is watching
him. He continues to walk as if he's crossing the street. Du knows
exactly what's going on, so he follows right behind E, until they get
to the other side.*

**"Yo, did you see that bitch? She chilling with this nigga,
fronting hard driving his shit. She even has the whole Mark
Cross outfit on. I put her down on that shit. She never heard of
Mark Cross until I took her to the Mall that day."**

*Du doesn't reply he just listens. He can see that E is really
hurt, that's why he hasn't made fun of the situation. Du has never
seen E take a girl so serious.*

*Everyone crowds around Cool Breeze as he gets out of the
car. They're shaking hands with him and hugging him like he's the
President. He stands there smiling, with a mouth full of gold teeth.
You can tell he loves every bit of the attention he's getting. This has
ruined E's night.*

"Are you ready, Du?"

"Whenever you are."

*They're on their way crossing the street when they notice a
blue Bonneville slowly pass them.*

"You know who that was in the Bonneville, right?" E
asks.

"Nah, who was it?"

"Buck-Wild and his crew," E replies.

"You know it's time to leave now!" says Du.

*Buck-Wild is a problem. He's a straight terror. Whenever
he's around that means trouble. He does everything from robbery to
extortion, and he has a pack of wolves that will do anything he tells
them to do.*

By the time they get back to the entrance Buck-Wild is

already out of the car. He slowly strolls around, not speaking to any one just giving everybody long hard stares. He looks like he just crawled out of a cave or something. Here it is summertime and he's walking around with a long sleeve thermal shirt on, tight as can be. He has muscles busting out everywhere. He has on dirty jean shorts and suede Timberlands with no shoestrings in them. To top it off, he has on a thick, black, wool skullcap on his head.

E and Du get in Du's car and drive toward Elizabeth Ave.
"Before we go home take one more spin around the block, and see if we can find some late night. I'm horny as hell!" says E.

Du circles the block. They see two young girls walking down the street.
"Hold up, hold up, what's that right there?" E asks. "Pull over and hit the horn!"

(Beep, Beep, Beep,) **"What up baby? Where ya'll headed?" E asks.**

"Home!" the first girl shouts.

"C'mon, where ya'll live?" E asks.

"That's alright, we live right around the corner!" shouts the second girl.

"You sure?"

"Yeah we're sure, bye," says the second girl.

"Fuck them!" Du shouts. *They immediately pull off.*

As they're approaching the corner the light turns red. While they're waiting for the light to turn green, a car pulls up close behind them, but they aren't paying any attention to it. The light turns green, but before Du can pull off, his driver's side door flies open.

"Nigga, get the fuck out!" *Du hesitates, by this time another person is grabbing on the passenger door where E is. The person on Du's side is yanking and pulling on Du trying to drag him out of the car. Du is holding on for dear life. During the commotion a third person runs over and snatches Du's chain off his neck.*

"I said get the fuck out the car!" the man shouts again.

"Pull off!" E screams.

By this time one of the boys is standing at the front of the car aiming a gun at the windshield. Du gasses up and tries to go around him.

*They recognize the gunman's face; it's Buck-Wild.
Buck-Wild fires two shots* **Boom! Boom!** *The windshield shatters. That doesn't stop Du. He continues to drive full speed.*

Through the rear view mirror Du can see the Bonneville getting closer. **Smack!** *They have rammed their car into Du's car, then* **Smack!** *They ram it again. Du turns the corner. He loses control. Now the Bonneville is side by side with them on E's side. The passenger is hanging out the window* **Boom! Boom! Boom! Boom!** *The passenger fires four shots, all four hitting Du's car door. Then finally Du gets a stretch on them and they back off.*

"**Do you see them?**" **E asks.**

"**Nah, they backed off. Du replies.**

"**Them niggas tried to carjack us!**" **E says** *nervously, while still trying to catch his breath.*

"**He was scheming the whole time, that's why he was staring at us like that," says Du.**

"**Word up," E agrees. "Go to my house so we can take a look at the car," E suggests.**

"**I know it's fucked up. I felt all the shots hit the car," says Du.**

"**That motherfucker was trying to kill us!**" **E shouts.**
"**The other one snatched my chain," says Du,** *sounding disappointed.*

"**Fuck that chain, you're still here and they didn't get your car.**"

"**Yeah, you right. It's these rims. We shouldn't have gone down there anyway. You know that's the car jack capitol.**"

When they reach E's house, they pull in the back yard to check the car. "**That was some big shit he had!**" **E shouts,** *as he looks at the four big holes in the door.*

"**If one of those shots would have hit us; boy, we would have been out of here," says Du.**

"**Hell yeah!**" **E agrees.** "**Leave it back here; just catch a cab home.**"

"**Alright,**" **Du replies.**

They proceed upstairs to call Auto Cab Company.

CHAPTER 10

The next night

The supervisor just unexpectedly laid all the temporary employees off because the workload had been cut down.

"**Damn, Flaco, I'm never going to be able to pay my way through school like this,**" **Tony says** *with a disappointing tone.* "**So what are you going to do now, Flaco?**"

"**I don't know yet, Poppy. If I go back to New York I'm finished. I'll come up with something.**"

After they pack up all their belongings, they walk outside to catch the number 1 Ivy Hill bus.

Neither of the two has spoken much during the long, bumpy, bus ride.

"**Next stop!**" **Flaco yells.** *His stop is first. Tony has to ride all the way downtown Newark and transfer to the 34 Bloomfield.* "**Yo, be good poppy! Here's my number, stay in touch with me.**"

As the bus pulls off Tony watches Flaco walk away from the bus. He starts laughing to himself when he thinks about, how Flaco had everybody fooled. Shortly after that Tony dozes off.

At the same time somewhere across town, it's 7 am, and E's cellular phone is ringing.

Ring, ring! "**Yo?**" **E answers.**

"**Hello, can I speak to E Boogie?**"

"**Speaking, who is this?**"

"**Isha, Aisha,**" *says the voice.*

E thinks he's dreaming. He's so anxious to find out what she's calling for, but he doesn't want to sound too desperate though.

"**Yeah and?**"

"I'm calling to find out if you are alright," Aisha claims.

"Yeah I'm alright, why wouldn't I be?" he asks sarcastically.

"I heard about last night," Aisha admits. "Everyone was talking about some kids in an orange CRX got shot and carjacked."

"Nah, we didn't get shot or jacked! They tried to get us though. They were surprised when we started shooting back," E lies.

"Oh yeah?" Aisha asks.

"So, you did see me last night, huh?"

"How could I miss you in that bright ass car?"

"Whatever! I saw you too; you was chilling, driving your man shit," says E.

"My man? That's not my man. That's my brother," Aisha replies.

"Your brother?"

"Yeah, that's my older brother. You thought that was my man?"

E feels so relieved. "I didn't know what to think.

"Anyway, I told you I didn't have a man!"

"Aisha, is it anyway I can make up to you for that night?"

"I don't know, I'll think about it," Aisha says, *with a sarcastic tone.* "By the time you pick me up from work today, I'll know exactly what I want you to do."

"Alright, anything Aisha, word up, anything you want."

"I get off at 6:00 today. I want you here at 5:50," she demands.

"I'll be there at 5:30. We're going to start off on the right track this time." *E laughs.*

As the weeks go by E and Aisha grow closer together. Wherever you see E, you see Aisha. They dress alike and everything. E has even dumped all his other girls.

Du is laying low. He only comes out every now and then.

He isn't sure if Buck- Wild is coming back for him.

As for Tony, he just stays around the house hoping someone will call him back for one of the 100 jobs he has applied for. He is starting to get frustrated and his College dreams are starting to look like they're further down the road.

CHAPTER 11

Tony and Du are at it again, playing the video game.
"That's it for me. I'm tired, I'm going home. We've been playing this stupid game for six hours," says Du.

"Damn, it doesn't seem that long," Tony replies. "This is normal for me. This is all I do all day now. I'm a professional video game player." Tony says, *in a joking manner.* "I can't believe this shit. I'm supposed to be in Virginia, but instead I'm up here playing video games all got damn day. Thanks to my piece of shit ass father."

"You'll be alright," Du claims, *trying to comfort Tony.*

"I don't know man, I feel bad as hell sitting here eating up all the food, while moms down there crying over light bills. I can't take too much more of this shit. I'm a grown ass man. This shit doesn't suppose to be happening like this," Tony says, *as he wipes the tears that are sliding down his face.*

"What are you going to do?" Du asks.

"That's what I called you over here for," Tony replies. "I need a big favor from you."

"Anything! What do you need, is it money?"

"Nah, bigger than that. I need you to put me on my feet."

"Put you on your feet how?" *Du can't believe what Tony is asking him to do. He's asking him to give him weed to sell. Tony isn't a drug dealer. What is he thinking about, Du asks himself.* "Tony, you talking stupid!"

"Du, I'm serious man. I need you. You know if I didn't need you, I wouldn't ask you."

"I know Tony, but I can't do that. I don't want to see

57

you go out like that. You got too much going for you, besides you're like my little brother."

"So you are going to let your little brother starve?"

"Chill out Tony, let me talk to E, and see what he say about this."

"Du, this ain't about E. I didn't ask E, I asked you," Tony states. "This is about you and me. Either you're going to do it, or you're not. It's that simple."

"Let me sleep on it," Du insists. "Tomorrow we'll hook back up.

"Alright sleep on it, but don't oversleep.

Du leaves.

All night long Tony can't get a wink of sleep, wondering if Du will do the favor for him.

As soon as 8 a.m. comes Tony beeps Du. Du never returns the call. He decides to call his house, but he doesn't get an answer. He even called E. He didn't answer either.

Weeks pass and Tony hasn't heard anything from E or Du. He calls both of them at least five times a day everyday. This is unusual. Tony knows they are ducking him so they don't have to do him the favor.

Tony doesn't know what to do or who to turn to. He's holding onto his last unemployment check. He's about to lose hope until, "Flaco!" he blurts out. "I'll call Flaco!

Tony hates to do this but he has to do something. He calls Flaco and they set up a meeting place and a time.

"What's up Poppy? You said you have a problem, what is it?" Flaco asks.

"Yeah Flaco, I have a problem." *Tony pauses for a few seconds.* "Flaco, I hate to come to you like this, but I need some cocaine. I need money bad," Tony admits. "I have things to do. You know I want to go to school, but I can't find a job to pay my way through."

"Poppy, I don't want to fuck with that shit. You know my situation."

"Please Flaco," Tony begs. "I need you just this one time. I don't have anyone else to turn to. My boys turned their backs on me."

"Come on poppy; please don't make me do this. I don't want to get back involved in that."

"Please Flaco," Tony begs. "If you don't want to do it just hook me up with somebody else."

"Damn Poppy, I should have never told you!"

Flaco pauses, then he slowly starts dialing numbers on the pay phone they're standing by. **"Hola, Donde esta Pablo? Si, es Jose. Si."** *He holds a small conversation in Spanish then he turns to Tony and says,* **"I'll hook you up with my brother. How much do you want?"**

"I got three hundred dollars," says Tony, *while waving his unemployment money.* "What can I get with that?"

"I can get you a half an ounce with that," Flaco replies.

Tony doesn't know the difference between a half an ounce and a hole in the wall, but he can't admit that to Flaco.

"Poppy, I don't want no trouble. I did you a favor, that's it. I'll call you and we'll meet back here later."

"Thanks Flaco!"

CHAPTER 12

The rest of the day Tony tries to figure out how he will move the cocaine. When he finally gets the work from Flaco he calls his aunt to test it. She's his mother's sister. She won't tell. As long as she gets a free high she'll keep her mouth shut.

Tony hands his aunt a small piece of cocaine. She puts the small pebble sized rock inside a small glass jar. She then adds baking soda and water. After that she puts the flame from her lighter to the bottom of the glass jar.

"Got damn nephew, this shit come back fat as hell. Where did you get this? Do you have a lot of it?"

She's so amazed that, she asks question after question without waiting for the answer. She then places the rock inside her glass pipe. She lights it and takes a blast. She takes a long pull. Her eyes are almost popping out of her head.

"It tastes good too. Do you see how clear the water is? That means it's pure cocaine, no cut, and it didn't take long to get hard," she claims.

Tony doesn't have a clue what she's talking about. The most important thing is the fact that she said it was good.

Immediately after taking the blast she starts talking excessively. Her mouth starts twitching from side to side. Auntie dashes out of the door. She runs outside and starts bringing customers to him. He doesn't have time to bag it up, so he just breaks off little pieces for them as they come.

He has made a week's worth of work money in a half of an hour. He can't believe it.

After about two hours he packs up and goes home. He doesn't want to be greedy.

The next day is even better. Tony has the little blue plastic bags packed all the way to the top. He's selling them for ten dollars a bag. His Aunt is bringing sales from everywhere. For every five sales she brings in, he gives her one for herself.

All Tony has to do is sit in the living room of Auntie's apartment, while she brings the customers in. The customers don't buy one. They buy six or eight. Some even buy ten at a time. The money is coming so fast that he doesn't have time to count it. He just stuffs it in his pockets.

"Tony, my girl right here wants to know if you'll let her get eleven for a hundred?"

"I'm down to my last eight," Tony replies. **"I'm almost sold out."**

"Give them here!" Auntie shouts.

That's it. The half-ounce of powder is gone. He will have to call Flaco and re-up. Tony is amazed at how fast he got rid of it. He knows if things keep going at this speed he will be in Virginia, at school in no time at all.

Weeks have flown by and Tony hasn't bothered to call his boys. He's still angry with them for ducking him, but he misses being around them. After all, he has been around them ever since kindergarten.

Besides that everything is going good, Tony is making more money than he has ever seen. The only problem is, his competition on the corner is getting jealous. They're tired of the customers walking past them to get to him. They even threatened to beat his aunt up if she doesn't stop running sales.

"Nephew, them boys mad at me out there!" Auntie shouts, *as she walks through the door.*

"What did they say to you?"

"The same thing from earlier, how am I going to let that schoolboy come around here and set up shop?"

"Schoolboy?"

"But one of them got real nasty with me. He got in my face and said he was going to slap the shit out of me. When

Reemie comes home I am going to make him fuck him up."

Reemie is her only son. He's been in jail for ten years. He killed an old lady in an accident, while he was driving a stolen car. The judge sentenced him to juvenile life when he was sixteen years old. He was supposed to be home three years ago but he stays in so much trouble.

"You knew Reemie was on his way home didn't you?" she asks.

"Nah, I didn't."

"Yeah he should be home in a couple of months."

The rest of the day was big business. Auntie ran in and out all day long.

"Auntie, I'm about to go home."

"Why are you leaving so early? It's only nine o clock, shit about to start jumping, checks came out today. Motherfuckers are going to be spending all night," she explains, *trying to convince Tony to stay out.*

"I'm tired," says Tony.

"Well leave some with me, because I'll be up all night. It ain't no need letting that money go to somebody else."

Tony thinks about it. The idea sounds good, but he knows if he leaves something she will smoke it up. "Nah, that's alright. I want to have something to last for tomorrow. Tomorrow is the real check day."

"Can you leave me with four? I'll work it off as soon as we get started tomorrow. I promise."

"Here," says Tony, *as he passes the four baggies to Auntie.*

"Thanks Nephew!"

"Later Auntie!" Tony shouts, *as he walks out the door.*

She ignores him. She has already started cooking the rock up.

By the time he gets to the staircase in the hallway, he sees two boys coming in.

"What's up schoolboy?" the first boy asks, *while the second one pushes Tony against the wall and aims a small handgun at his chest.*

"Empty your motherfucking pockets!" the second boy shouts. "Where's the money?"

Tony begins pulling money from everywhere, without hesitation. He also hands them all the plastic bags of rock he has left.

"Is that all you got?" the second boy asks.

"Yeah that's it!" Tony yells.

"Don't make me check you. If I check you and I find something else, I'm going to bust you."

"That's it, I swear," Tony replies.

"Yo, check his shoes," says the first boy. "Make him take off his shoes." *Tony kicks off his shoes instantly.*

"Listen schoolboy," says the second boy. "You ain't from around here, so you're not going to be coming around here getting money. Do you hear me?"

"Yeah," Tony replies.

The boys then back up out of the hallway, and Tony busts into the living room. His heart is pounding. He's scared to death. Tony has never been robbed before. "Auntie! They robbed me, they robbed me!"

"Calm down nephew," she replies calmly. "Who robbed you?"

"Them boys from the corner! They put the gun to my chest and robbed me!"

"Stop screaming like a bitch, that's part of the game! It's called occupational hazard!" Auntie shouts, *as she sits there high as a kite, not even interested in what Tony is talking about. The only thing on her mind is smoking that pipe.*

After that Tony took a couple of days off, but it wasn't long before he was back doing his thing. A crack head came through with a .22 automatic handgun. Tony gave him five plastics for it. He never takes it off his waist while he's in the apartment. Tony doesn't want to hurt anyone but he can't let any one hurt him either.

CHAPTER 13

Tony waits impatiently for Flaco to arrive. He's so anxious to get back on the block, because money is coming. He has been waiting in McDonalds for forty-five minutes so far.

While looking out the window Tony sees the white Chevy Spectrum pull up and park in the lot. Tony walks out nonchalantly and jumps in the backseat. Flaco is in the passenger seat and his brother is driving.

"Flaco, what's up?"

"What's up poppy? Here's the work right here," says Flaco, as he hands Tony the sandwich bag full of cocaine.

"One-piece right?" Tony asks. "You know I don't like that powder shit, Flaco."

"Yeah, it's only one piece. That'll be $2,100," says Flaco.

Tony quickly hands Flaco the money. Tony has the money stacked in hundreds. In total, there are twenty-one stacks with a rubber band wrapped around them. After he hands over the money, Flaco's brother starts shaking his head no, and speaking Spanish

"Mucho problemo con la policia." That's all Tony can make out.

"What did he say?" Tony asks Flaco.

"He said never carry your money like that, because you'll get a lot of problems with the police if they stop you. When they see money stacked like that they automatically think it's drug money."

"Alright, next time I'll do it different," Tony claims.

"Later poppy, be safe."

Tony already has his empty bottles, now he has to go bag up. Tony has switched from plastic bags to small glass bottles. Now he *really has the apartment rocking.*

Tony paid a crack head three bottles to let him bag up in his apartment.

Tony is sitting at the kitchen table. In front of him is a plate, two razors, eight boxes of empty vials, and one hundred grams of cocaine.

He sits there looking at the rock. He can't believe he has worked his way up to one hundred grams.

As he chops the rock, the crack head just sits there watching, looking like a thirsty dog on a hot summer day.

"Here, stop staring at me like that!" Tony yells, *as he hands the crack head a tiny crumb of the rock.*

The crack head cooks the rock up. Tony has seen his Aunt get high lots of times, but this crack head is doing something different. Before the rock gets hard, he puts the liquid cocaine inside a syringe and he immediately shoots himself in the arm with the needle. After poking himself he nods out and then, **BOOM!** *He falls onto the floor with the needle still in his arm.*

Tony jumps up and starts shaking him. Tony thinks he's dead until he awakens and looks him in the eyes. **"Got damn that shit good!"**

Tony chops the rock and starts stuffing tiny crumbs inside the little bottles. He's rushing, trying to get out of there. He doesn't want to see the crack head poke himself again.

Tony finally finishes. He bags up 790-dime bottles. It took him almost five hours. His fingers are so numb. He even has little cuts in his fingertips from the dull razors popping off the rock.

"Here you go!" Tony shouts, *as he hands the man three more vials. He immediately takes off to the apartment.*

Hours later

Tony has been banging the jumbo dimes all day. He's making a killing! Tired now from all the hustle and bustle, he lays there on the couch, with his feet kicked up watching television,

65

when   Auntie comes busting in with another girl. This is a kind of young girl. She has a pretty face and she's thick. When you look in her face you can tell she's kind of run down.

"**Nephew, I got somebody who wants to meet you,**" says **Auntie. "Come here, Sherry!**" *The girl stands there looking shy. She slowly walks over to Tony.* "**Nephew, this is Sherry, Sherry this is my Nephew.**" *Auntie walks into the bedroom, leaving Sherry and Tony standing there face to face. Tony is clueless. He's trying to figure out what is going on, until Sherry speaks.*

"**Nephew, you got them jumbo dimes right?**"

"**Yeah,**" Tony answers, *still looking clueless.*

"**I wanted one, but I don't have the money right now,**" says Sherry.

"**You look young, how old are you?**" Tony asks. *He's shocked by what she just said to him.*

"**I'm 18, but that's neither here nor there,**" she replies.

"**I'm sorry but I don't do the credit thing,**" Tony admits.

"**No baby, I'm not looking for credit. I wanted to know is it anything I could do for you?**"

"**Do for me, like what?**" *Now Tony is totally confused.*

"**Like a favor, you know, head or some pussy.**" *The words head or pussy echo in his head so many times until his dick gets hard. He stands there in shock, with no response.* "**Well Nephew, do you want some of this fat ass or what?**" **she says arrogantly,** *as she pulls her shorts down to her knees and turns to show him her ass.*

Eighteen, my age, selling pussy is all Tony keeps thinking. "**C, c, c'mon,**" he stutters. *His heart pounds in his chest.*

Sherry starts pulling her clothes off. Then she pushes him back onto the couch. She drops down on her knees, and unzips Tony's pants. She pulls out his rock hard dick, and begins sucking his balls first. Then she looks up and asks him, "**Do you have one on you?**"

Tony quickly hands her the bottle. She takes the top off and sprinkles a little powder on Tony's dick. She licks him up and down before she starts to suck away. Tony sits there laid back, with both of his hands palming her big ass. She starts sucking harder and faster. Tony is almost ready to explode. He grabs the back of her head and starts fucking her in the mouth. He has to be pumping at least 100 miles per hour. He explodes in her mouth. **"Aghhhh!"** *She licks him dry.*

"Sherry get it all, I didn't miss a drop. C'mon get up, I want to fuck now!" she shouts.

Tony sits there feeling dirty and disgusted. **"Nah, nah, that's alright. Here you go, here is another one for you."**

"What, are you scared of this big ass?"

"Nah, I'm alright."

At this moment Tony hates himself for what he has done. He can't believe the young girl sucked him off for a lousy bottle of cocaine.

As the girl puts her clothes on, Auntie walks in laughing. **"Nephew, how was she?"**

He's so ashamed he can't look his Aunt in the face.

Sherry and Auntie haul ass out the door. Tony then realizes that his Aunt has set him up with the girl just so she can get a free hit.

He gets up, locks the door and begins counting his money. Today is the best day Tony has had. Today he scored $3,700. The customers love the jumbo dimes.

He stuffs the money in his underwear, takes his gun off his waist, slides one bullet into the chamber, takes the safety off and walks out the door. Something about that gun makes Tony feel like a real gangster.

CHAPTER 14

It's a beautiful August day. It's 80 degrees, with lots of sun. E and Du are coming down Rt. 280 doing 110 miles an hour on their motorcycles.

They have been riding all morning. They just bought the Ninjas two days ago. Du sold his car, and E gave his to his man J.J.

J.J. is E's runner, that's who sells the weed for him on the block.

E pulls over on First Street, across from the Newark Slip Co. (N. and S.), and waits for Du to catch up.

Du pulls up seconds later.

"Where are you headed now?" Du mumbles, *from under the helmet.*

"I'm going to meet him," E replies.

"You got the money with you?" Du asks.

"Yeah, it's right here, E replies, *while tapping the trunk space on the back of his seat.*

"Alright, come by my house when you finish."

"Bet!"

Du speeds off and E follows right behind him. E is riding like a nut, zipping in and out of traffic. He hasn't stopped for one red light.

As he pulls up to the meeting place he notices his man is already there. But there is something different; his man is outside the car talking to another guy.

As E gets closer he realizes this isn't the guy who normally drives for his man. E pulls up, but not too close. He doesn't want to interrupt their conversation.

The other guy looks familiar, but E can't place his face. The other guy is doing most of the talking, while E's man stands there just listening.

"You been telling me the same shit for six months! Stop making me promises, if you're not going to deliver."

"Nah man, shit been rough for me. You don't understand," E's man explains.

Then it dawns on E who the other guy is. It's Buck- Wild. E sneakily rides across the street so Buck- Wild won't recognize him. He can still hear the conversation because Buck- Wild is starting to yell now.

"You been telling me, that you're going to hit me off ever since I first came home!" Buck Wild yells. "You playing me the fuck out! I'm tired of chasing you around, then when I finally catch up with you, it's yo Buck I got you. I have been home for six months nigga, hit me!"

For the first time ever, E can see fear in his man's eyes. He isn't such a tough guy after all. He's just standing there letting Buck- Wild point in his face and poke him in his chest.

"I really don't have it like that."

"You don't have it like that?" Buck Wild asks sarcastically. "Nigga you selling massive weed, and you're going to stand here and lie to my face like that. Do you think I'm a joke?"

Before E's man can respond Buck- Wild pulls a gun from under his shirt.

E pulls up the block a little further.

"Come on, Buck?"

"Come on my ass, I'm tired of playing games with you. Give me something right now. Give me some dough, some weed, or something."

"I don't have shit," E's man whispers.

"Motherfucker you got something, you riding around here in a brand new Mercedes! You know what, run your motherfucking pockets!"

While aiming the gun at his face, Buck starts going through his pockets. He pulls out a stack of money.

"I thought you didn't have shit!" Buck shouts. "I thought you didn't have shit!" BOOM! *He shoots him in the chest.*

"Aghhhh!" E's man screams.

E is petrified. He's so scared that he can't move. Fear has him paralyzed.

BOOM! BOOM! BOOM*! He shoots three more times. E's man slides down the wall, leaving a bloodstain on the wall behind him. He lays there twisted on the concrete.*

E pulls off like a bat out of hell, looking through the mirrors making sure nobody is behind him, dipping in and out of traffic. A bus almost nails him as he zooms through the red light, not looking either way.

He's not sure which way he should go. He doesn't want to go home because he doesn't know who saw him at the scene. E wonders if his man is dead. That's the worst shit he has ever seen in his life.

E finally gets to JJ's house. He parks the bike and jumps in the car with JJ. The only person that he will ever tell what he just witnessed, will be Du.

CHAPTER 15

For the past couple of days things have been going good for Tony. He's making so much money. Two guys from the corner have even taken work from him. You know the saying (if you can't beat them, join them.) He doesn't need his aunt to run sales anymore because the customers either come directly to the apartment, or they see one of the two guys on the corner. Between him and his two runners, he averages about $6,000 a day.

Everything was going fine until Auntie caught an attitude and told Tony's mother.

Tony's mother busts in the room while Tony is playing the video game. **"Turn the game off!" his Mom shouts. "I want to talk to you."** *Tony continues to play the game as if he didn't hear her.*

"Motherfucker, do you hear me talking to you? Turn the got damn game off!"

This catches Tony's attention. His mother rarely speaks to him like that. He can see the rage in her face. He knows she means business. **"Ma, what's up?" Tony asks,** *as he turns the game off.*

"Are you selling drugs?"

"Huh?"

"You heard me, are you selling drugs?"

"Ma, who told you that?"

"Don't worry about it; just answer my question," *Mom says with a firm voice.*

"Ma, who told you that?" Tony asks again.

"I'm asking the fucking questions!" she screams. "I'm going to ask you again. Are you selling drugs?" *Tony doesn't respond.* **"Tony, I didn't raise a drug dealer. I busted my ass to**

make sure you have, and this is how you repay me? Tony where did I go wrong? Tell me," she begs, *as the tears roll down her face.*

Tony's eyes start to water. "Ma, I'm tired of being broke. I didn't know what to do. You know how bad I want to go to school. It seems like every time I turn around it's another obstacle in the way. I didn't want to stress you out; I knew you couldn't afford to pay for it. So I figured I could make some fast money this way."

"Tony, who are you working for? Is it E or Du?"

"I'm not working for anyone. I would never work for anyone. I am my own man, and anything I do will be for me!"

"Tony, you have to stop! Please stop! If you don't you will have to leave my house!" she screams, *as she walks out the room.*

Crack head bitch, Tony thinks to himself. He can't believe that his aunt would ruin the bond he and his mother have, all for a blast. He's determined to never fuck with his aunt ever again.

CHAPTER 16

The word is all over town that E's man had been murdered.
The murderer no one reveals. E is not sure if they know and are
keeping it a secret out of fear, or they just really don't know who
killed him.

It's been days and no one has called for the money E and Du
owed his man for the weed he fronted them before he got murdered.
They decide to flip the money in New York. They're going to start
selling cocaine. If someone calls for the money they'll give it to
them, but until then they have 10,000 free dollars.

They have been thinking about switching to cocaine for
quite a while now. Everybody knows that cocaine is where the real
money is. Neither one of them has any connections, but they know a
crack head that claims he knows where to get the best cocaine from.

The four of them ride to New York, E, Du, Aisha and the
crack head. The crack head drives because neither one of them
knows how to get there. The spot is on 162nd and Broadway. The
crack head parks on 158th Street.

"Why are you parking all the way around here?" E
asks.

"Just in case the police are watching they won't see the
Jersey license plates," the crack head explains. "Du, you walk
up ahead. E, you and Aisha walk together. I'll cross the street.
Ya'll follow my lead. We all can't walk together that'll draw too
much attention," he explains. "E, when you get to the corner
go in the bodega and a get few items, like cookies, cereal, milk,
some fruit, a half-gallon of orange juice and some crazy glue.
Oh shit, I almost forgot; get me a shaker and a stem." *(The*
shaker is a small glass bottle used to cook the cocaine in, and a

stem is another term for a crack pipe)

> *E doesn't ask any questions. He's so busy trying to remember all the items he asked for.*
>
> *After he gets the items he walks to the spot like he was instructed to do.*
>
> *As they walk to the building everyone is nervous except the crack head. He has done this a million times.*
>
> *Once they get to the entrance a crowd of Spanish boys attack them like vultures, grabbing and pulling on them. I got fish scale is what they all are screaming.*
>
> *When the crack head presses the doorbell, someone immediately buzzes him in. They walk up the stairs to the second floor.*
>
> *When they get to the door and knock, the peephole clicks, and the door opens immediately. When they enter, there is a short Spanish man standing in the doorway with a .357 magnum in his hand. He checks everyone one by one. First he checks the crack head; next in line is Du, then E. When he gets to Aisha, he doesn't pat her down, he just instructs her to lift up her blouse. As she's walking away she squeezes E's hand so tight. Her palms are sweaty. She's so nervous.*
>
> *The crack head tells them to have a seat in the living room, and to be quiet and let him do the talking.*
>
> *The crack head makes himself right at home in the raggedy apartment. There are only two chairs and a television in the living room. In the kitchen there is a table with no chairs, a refrigerator and a triple beam scale on the countertop.*
>
> *The crack head walks to the refrigerator and grabs a Heineken. He then whispers to the man standing at the scale,* **"Poppy, where is my GP?"**
>
> *No one knows what that means. The man at the scale hands him a little powder in aluminum foil. The crack head then sniffs the powder, and the residue that's left, he licks off the foil.*
>
> **"Poppy, these are my nephews, take care of them."**
> **"Ok, ok, poppy, you know me long time,"** *says the man*

74

operating the scale. *(He speaks in broken English).*

"How much, Poppy? What are ya'll getting?" the crack head asks.

"How much is it a gram?" E asks.

"Twenty-four dollars a gram," the Spanish man replies.

"Du, what do you want to get? Do you want to spend all of it?"

"Nah, just get 300 grams," Du replies.

"300 grams, Poppy!" E shouts.

The Spanish man grabs one of the pillows from the couch, and unzips it. He sticks his hand inside the pillow, and comes out with two plastic bags filled with cocaine. He gives the crack head one small rock from each bag. The crack head hurries into the bathroom to sample it. He has to determine which bag has the better quality of cocaine in it.

Five minutes later he walks out wide-eyed. **"This one," he says**, while pointing to the bag with the biggest rocks in it.

The Spanish man places 300 grams on the scale. Actually the scale reads 301. The bag weighs a gram by itself.

While the Spanish man is counting the money, the crack head grabs the container of orange juice and opens it up. He breaks the seal across the top. He pours out almost half of the juice. Then he puts the cocaine filled plastic bag into six more plastic bags. He places the big ball of plastic bags into the orange juice container. Finally he crazy glues the sealing back together and puts the container back in the bag with the rest of the groceries.

"The money is right," says the Spanish man. "$7,200," he adds.

"What about me?" the crack head asks. "My nephews spent a lot of money, you have to take care of me!" *The Spanish man hands him seven grams for himself.*

They walk out of the building in the same order they came in. E and Aisha are carrying the groceries just like the crack head instructed. They all make it to the car safely.

After they cross the bridge, he starts driving recklessly.

"**Slow down motherfucker, police are all over!**" **E shouts,** *as they near the Fort Lee exit.*

"**Sit back, I got this, I have been doing this since you were a baby and I have never been caught.**"

The word caught, sounds off in all of their heads. The crack head slows down as he approaches some troopers near exit 68 Ridgefield exit. (Cocaine alley is what police nicknamed that area; that is the area where State Troopers usually catch drug dealers coming back from New York.)

They breeze by them. After that it's all smooth sailing. They make it back to Newark safe and sound.

CHAPTER 17

Tony doesn't use the apartment anymore ever since his aunt told his mother about him selling drugs. He has nowhere to stash the drugs, so he can't work. He has to direct all his sells to the two guys he has working for him. He just sits on the porch all day while his two boys run around making a killing. The other guys on the block hate him because they feel like he's trying to take over. They don't even know his name. He's referred to as Nephew because of his aunt.

"Nephew, can I get twelve for a hundred?" The crack head screams.

"Yo, get twelve," Nephew shouts to his two runners.

The customers run back and forth. Give me a clip (10 bottles), give me sixteen, give me two clips. That's how the money is coming. Tony is making more money than he could ever imagine. Tony has been outside for only three hours and he has already made $2,000.

"Nephew!" shouts the voice.

"What's up, how many?" Tony asks.

"Nah, nah, baby I don't want nothing. I need to talk you." Tony stands up immediately, remembering that time the guys robbed him.

"Talk to me about what?" he asks defensively.

"First of all, let me introduce myself. My name is Rick. I'm sure you've heard of me. I pretty much run things around here. Don't nothing move around here with out me knowing about it."

"Yeah and?"

"Yeah and, I heard you moving a lot of work around here and you ain't paying no taxes."

"Taxes?" Tony asks, without a clue of what he's talking about.

"Yeah taxes, I'm Uncle Sam around here, and you have to pay up."

"Yeah," Tony replies sarcastically.

"I mean, don't look at it like it's free money for me. Look at it like protection for you. You hit me and you don't have to worry about nothing. No stick-ups, no nothing. If a nigga even look at you wrong, I'll handle him." Tony looks at him with a blank look on his face. "I normally charge $500 a week. That's what all the jokers around here give me every Friday, but being that you not from around here, I'm going to need $1, 500 a week from you."

"$1,500?"

"Yeah $1,500, and you've been getting money for some time now without paying Uncle Sam so I need a security deposit from you. Give me $1,000 today and on Friday you give me the normal $1,500."

"Are you serious?"

"Do I look like I'm playing?"

"Yo, I don't have a thousand dollars today and I am not going to have fifteen hundred on Friday."

"Cool, then you can't be out here."

"Oh, I'll be out here!" says Tony with bitterness in his voice.

Rick starts stepping closer to Tony while Tony backs away from him. Rick draws his gun and continues to inch up on Tony. Tony continues to back up. Tony discreetly tries to reach for his gun. Rick realizes what he's trying to do, so he fires a shot, BANG! Tony flinches and tries to cover his head with his forearm. Then BANG! Rick fires again. This shot hits Tony in the elbow. He's in so much shock that he doesn't even know that he's hit.

Finally, he gets to his gun, he aims at Rick. He closes his eyes and squeezes. POP! POP! Rick back peddles down the stairs and fires another shot, BANG! When he gets to the bottom of the stairs he turns around and runs off.

78

*Tony fires another shot **POP**! To Tony's surprise he hits Rick in the shoulder, but Rick hasn't stopped. Tony chases behind him and fires again. POP! This time he misses him. He squeezes again. POP! This shot hits Rick in the hip. The impact of the bullet spins him around and knocks him off his feet.*

Tony stops in amazement. His face goes blank. He's in total shock.

Seconds later he comes back to his senses. He looks down at the blood that's covering his clothes, realizing that he has been hit. He then takes off running the opposite way.

CHAPTER 18

Tony is alright. The bullet went straight through without hitting his bone or anything major. It didn't do any damage.

As for Rick, he has a fractured shoulder and a broken hip. He's in the College Hospital (UMDNJ.) The police have him chained to the bed. He has a bunch of bench warrants.

Tony isn't worried about Rick. His main concern is his mother finding out about the shoot out. She would really kill him if she found out about that.

The police questioned him and let him go. He told them someone tried to rob him. At first they didn't believe him, until Auntie and some other crack heads came there with the same story. Auntie apologized for what she had done, and promised she wouldn't tell his mother about the shoot out.

Tony's two boys have come by the house to see him and give him the rest of the money they owed him. Before giving him the money, they tell him how everybody in town is on his dick, because he shot Rick. Everyone was tired of Rick, but no one had enough heart to do anything about it, so now everyone looks at Tony as if he's a hero.

They count the money out to Tony; $16,000, for three days of work. He tells them he has to re-up, and he will call them when he's ready.

After they leave, Tony reaches for his Timberland box from his closet. As he pulls the neat stacks from his box he begins counting. One, two, three, four, five, six, seven, eight, nine, ten, eleven, twelve, thirteen, fourteen, plus the sixteen his boys just gave him. Tony has accumulated $30,000. Thirty grand, he thinks to himself. It seems like the more money he stuffs into that Timberland box, the further away from college he is.

CHAPTER 19

The fall season has just come in, and it is already starting to get cold. Tony needed some wheels, so he went to the car auction and bought a 1985 Porsche 944. He only paid $9,000 for it. It's silver with black leather interior with chrome BBS rims.

With that car and the shooting, Tony is now a star in his neighborhood. Now everybody and their mother want to work for him. He added three more players to his team. Now he has a starting five line up, as he calls it, comparing his team to a basketball team.

Auntie, she doesn't have to run sales anymore. All she has to do is hold the work in her apartment. He calls her his team manager. His operation has picked up so much that Flaco can't believe it. The little schoolboy, who at one time begged him for a half a ounce, is now buying a half a kilo every 3 days.

As Tony pulls out of High Tech Car Wash on Central Ave, in East Orange, his car is looking brand new. The wax job brings the paint out. No one can guess his car is only an 85. Tires dripping armorall, you can't tell Tony anything.

As he pulls to the traffic light, everyone is staring at him. Girls are pulling side by side to see who is driving. They're hitting the horn and waving at him. He loves all the attention.

A gray Chevy Blazer pulls up on the side of him. The Blazer has tinted windows so it is impossible for Tony to see inside. He can tell that it is two dudes, because he can see their shadows.

They follow him block after block almost slamming into him everytime he stops. Tony begins to get nervous. He reaches under his seat, grabs his gun and puts it under his leg. He then turns the corner.

If they follow me around this corner, I'm going to start busting, he thinks to himself.

He turns and they turn. The Blazer pulls up on the side of him. He aims. The window slides down. To Tony's surprise it's E. Judging by the look on E's face, he's terrified.

"Hold up, this me!"

"I didn't know who the fuck you were. Stop playing so much. Get your mother fucking head shot off!"

Du pops up and says, "Tony, pull over."

Tony pulls over and gets out. He has on a full-length chocolate brown shearling with the hat to match, and some tall chocolate brown cracked leather, 40 below timberlands. They have never seen Tony looking so slick.

"Damn, Ronald McDonald!" E shouts.

"Listen; stop playing. Everything ain't a game," Tony replies.

"Whose car?" Du asks.

"Who driving?" Tony replies, *using the same line E used on him before.*

"Yo, about that shit that happened.

Du attempts to finish his sentence when Tony blurts out, "What shit?"

"You know, putting you on board. Man, I didn't."

Before he can finish Tony interrupts him. "Don't worry about it, that's a small thing to a giant."

"Damn Tony, you looking good!" says E. "What are you doing?"

"I'm doing me!" Tony answers sarcastically.

"Yeah, where you at?" Du asks.

"Around my aunt's way," Tony replies. "Come through and check me out."

"When?" Du asks.

"Whenever, if you don't see my car ask one of my little niggas where I'm at. Don't come around there asking for Tony. Ask for Nephew."

He shakes their hands, jumps back in the Porsche and peels off full speed. E and Du stand there, not knowing what has gotten into Tony. He acted so arrogant.

That can't be the famous (Nephew), they think to themselves.

CHAPTER 20

    Tony has been waiting in his new apartment all morning for the deliveryman to deliver his bed. One of Tony's customers owns the three family house. The customer lives in the basement and he rents the first floor to Tony. He's charging Tony close to nothing for rent because Tony always takes care of him. Tony gives him whatever he wants because he always pays back.

    Tony isn't moving out of his mother's house. He's going to use the apartment as his little hide out. He will bag up here, and take his little girls here instead of wasting money on hotels.

    The apartment already has a cheap kitchen set in it. Now all he needs is a big King size waterbed and he will be straight.

    He can't wait too much longer for the deliveryman because he has things to do. He has to meet Flaco and most important of all he has to pick something up for his mother's birthday. Tomorrow she will be turning 50 years old.

    He sits for another half hour before the deliveryman gets there. After receiving the bed, Tony heads out the door to meet Flaco.

CHAPTER 21

Tony is so anxious to give his mother her birthday gift that he could barely sleep last night. He knows she will be surprised. He just wants to show her how grateful he is to have a mom like her.

Just before he's about to lotion up, he lays his suit across the bed.

He's sure his mother will be shocked when he tells her he's going to church with her. He hasn't been to church in ten years. He bought a new suit and shoes yesterday at the mall just for this occasion.

As he reaches for his suit the phone rings. **Ring, ring!**
"Hello?" he answers.

"Hey, Tony!"

"Hello?"

"Yeah, Tony this is your father"

"Oh, what's up," Tony asks, *with a disappointing tone.*
What the hell does he want, Tony asks himself. This is the first time Tony has heard from his father, since the night he called and cursed him out.

"Nothing much Tony, what's up with you?"

"Nothing at all," Tony replies, *trying to keep his answers short.*

"Nothing new?" his Dad asks.

"Nope!"

"Are you sure, Tony?"

"Yeah, I'm sure."

"Are you positive?"

What is he trying to get at, Tony asks himself. **"Yep, positive!"**

"What are you doing with yourself?" his Dad asks.

"Nothing, just trying to survive," Tony replies.

"And how are you doing that?"

"However I can."

He pauses for a few seconds before asking the next question.

"So Tony you're not going to tell me about your new car?"

That's what he's been trying to get at, Tony thinks to himself. "What about it?"

"I don't know, anything you think I should know," his Dad replies sarcastically.

"There's nothing really to tell you about it."

"That Porsche is a reall expensive car, huh?" his Dad asks.

"Nah, not really," Tony replies.

"Oh yeah Tony, that Porsche is very expensive. How can you afford a car like that? What are you doing for a living? You must be flipping a lot of burgers!"

"Nah Pop, I'm not flipping burgers anymore. I been left that job."

"Oh yeah, so what are you doing now?"

"Nothing right now."

"Oh you're doing something. You can't afford a $100,000 car doing nothing, ah ah Tony. I know exactly what you're doing."

"I'm not doing anything," Tony lies.

"Tony, cut the shit. I know what you're doing. Tony, you better give that man his car back!"

"What man," Tony asks.

"Tony, you know what man. Give him his car back. You don't know what you're getting yourself into!"

"Dad, what man are you talking about? That's my car."

"Tony, give him that fucking car back! This is a serious business. Get out while you can. Give him his car back and tell him you don't want to work for him anymore!"

"Work for who? Who are you talking about? I don't work for anyone!"

"Tony, I'm telling you, he's never gonna let you out!"

"Tony, give him that car back!"

Tony looks at the clock, time is running out. His mother will be leaving out soon. "Pop, I have to go now. I'll call you later."

"Listen, Tony!"

"Pop, later, I have to run!"

"Tony listen!"

"Later Pop, I'll call you back!" Click!

He has some nerve. It's all his fault, now he wants me to stop, Tony thinks to himself.

Tony gets dressed and proceeds to his mother's room, with her present. He knocks on the door lightly. **Knock, knock.**

"Come in!" *Tony walks in smiling with the big box in his hands. Perfume fills the air in mom's room. She has the gospel station blasting. She's standing at the mirror putting on her lipstick. She only has on a bra and her slip. When mom looks at Tony her eyes light up instantly.*

"Happy Birthday Ma."

"Thank you baby. Look at you; you look like a grown man. Why are you all dressed up?"

"Ma, I am a grown man," Tony replies. "I'm going to church with you."

"You're going to church? Get out of here boy!" *Tony's mom knows how much he hates going to church.*

"Serious Ma, I'm going with you. Here open this," he says, *as he hands her the box.*

"Wow, this is a special birthday. I get a gift and you're going to church with me. That's two gifts in one."

As she opens the gift Tony stands there looking in her eyes. He can't wait to see the look on her face. She finally gets it open. To mom's surprise it's a full-length shiny black mink. Mom's face shows no sign of emotion.

Tony is   disappointed because his mom isn't reacting

the way he thought she would. She barely gave him a half a smile.
"Try it on," he suggests.

She tries it on. As she walks to the mirror she still isn't showing any sign of emotion.

"What's the matter Ma? You don't like it?"

"No dear, I love it but I can't accept it!" she says, *as she takes it off and hands it back to him.*

Tony's feelings are crushed. He doesn't understand what's happening. "What do you mean you can't accept it?"

"Tony, I thank you. The coat is beautiful. I love it, but I will not accept it."

"Ma, if you love it take it."

"Tony, you and I both know that coat came from drug money. I will not walk around here in that coat knowing how many people's lives were destroyed just to buy this coat. There are innocent babies out here hungry, because their parents bought drugs instead of food. Wives can't pay the rent because their husbands bought drugs with the rent money. You are taking advantage of their weaknesses, and you expect me to walk around with that coat on and rub it in their faces. No Tony, I will not!"

Tony sits quietly. He has never looked at it like that yet it makes a lot of sense.

"So, are you still going to church with me, or what?"
"Yes Ma."

Tony leaves out so his mother can finish getting dress. When he enters his room he slams the door behind him and throws the coat onto the floor. Tony thought he was doing something good, instead he made things worse then they already were.

"Tony, I'm ready!"

When Tony gets to the kitchen he grabs his car keys. Mom looks at him and says, "No baby, we're riding in my car. We can't pull up to the church in that car. The whole congregation will be talking about me and my drug-dealing son.

Tony can't take it anymore. "Ma, are you ashamed of me?"

She doesn't respond.

"Ma, answer me!"

"Tony, I pray for you everyday. I want you out of the streets. I can barely sleep at night, worried about you. A lot of nights I can't go to sleep until I hear you open the door, just to know that you made it home safely. Tony, do you realize every time the phone rings my heart starts pounding, thinking someone is calling to tell me that you're dead. Tony, what is it that you want?"

"Ma, I just want us to be happy."

"Well baby, I hope you get what you want because you stole any hope of happiness that I could ever have."

Tony is fighting back the tears.

As they walk out the door, Tony feels like he's forgetting something. Then he realizes that he doesn't have his gun on him. He feels naked without his gun. He hasn't been outside for months without it.

They barely talk as they're riding to church. His mom is just singing along with the songs that are playing on the gospel tape. Jesus is going to fix it; is the song she rewinds over and over again.

CHAPTER 22

It's 8pm; Tony is in Auntie's apartment napping, when she runs in yelling. "Nephew! Nephew!" *Tony awakes startled.* "Two, boys are out there looking for you. They're inside a jeep with tinted windows. I ain't never seen them before."

"What color jeep?"

"Grey,"

"Tell them to come in," *he demands.*

Auntie dashes out.

E and Du hesitantly walk in by themselves.

"What up?" **E shouts,** *while Du just glances around the apartment.*

"What's up fellas? I was up in here knocked the fuck out."

"Your aunt gave us a hard time. She kept saying she didn't know a Nephew. She must have thought we were cops or something," says Du.

"Nah, it ain't that, shit crazy as hell around here," Tony explains.

"Yo, shit is rocking out there," says E. "Them motherfuckers are going crazy out there. What ya'll selling?"

"Coke," Tony replies. "This is a dime spot."

"That's what I'm talking about," says E. "Yo Tony, how did you get out here? Did you know somebody?"

"Yeah, my aunt!"

"And then you just came out here and set up shop?" E asks.

"Yeah," Tony replies.

"Nigga you're crazy!" Du shouts.

"I ain't crazy, I gotta eat."

"Is it all right out there?" Du asks.

"What do you mean?" Tony questions.

"I mean the money, is shit coming?"

"Man, shit coming! I'm killing them. No lie, I make anywhere, from $7,500 to $8,500 a night on this block."

"Get the fuck outta here," says E.

"Word is bond, no lie."

"Got damn, you doing your thing!" Du shouts.

They sit on the porch for an hour or so. Tony wants to show them he isn't lying. They're amazed at how much money, Tony or (Nephew, as every body calls him) is making.

The whole time they've been sitting there, the block has been jumping. People are pulling up in all kinds of cars. All kinds of people pull up, even upper class people. Give me eight; give me twelve that's all you hear the whole time.

"We need some of that shit he got," E yells out to Du.

"Tony, where is your spot?" Du asks.

"Do you go in the 180's? I heard they got the best shit up there," E claims.

"Nah, I got a nice connect. He's over here. He brings it right to me."

"Yo, you gotta hook us up," E shouts.

"I'll hook ya'll up. The same way ya'll hooked me up, when I asked to be put on board."

"Tony, it wasn't like that," Du states. "I didn't want to be the cause of you running the streets."

"Forget about it," says Tony. "I understand now, but then... I was hating ya'll two motherfuckers."

They all laugh.

"Are ya'll still fucking with that garbage ass weed?

"Nah," Du replies.

What happened with that?"

They pause for a few seconds, before E replies, "That's a long story."

91

"So what spot do ya'll go to?"

"162nd and Broadway," says E.

"How much do ya'll pay?"

"Twenty-four dollars a gram," E replies.

"Twenty-four? I can get it at twenty-one," says Tony.

"Damn, you gotta bring us in," Du replies.

"I'll hook ya'll up, the only thing is; he's not into meeting a lot of people."

"That's cool, as long as we can get it, he ain't never gotta meet me," says Du.

"Word up!" E agrees.

"Let me know when ya'll are ready to flip again," says Tony. "Ya'll hungry? Let's go over to the Steak and Take and get something to eat." *They all jump in the truck.*

The fellas hang out for the rest of the night. They update each other about what's going on. In the little time they were apart, a lot of things have changed in all of their lives.

CHAPTER 23

---

*Tony is at High Tech Car Wash. He's standing there
watching the men dry his car off, when his phone begins ringing.*
"Hello!"
"Tony!"
"Yeah, who is this?"
"It's me motherfucker!" *This is E.*
"E, what's up baby?"
"Where are you? I need to kick it with you."
"I'm at the car wash. I'll come pick you up as soon as I
leave here."
"Alright," E replies.
*Tony begins to apply the armorall on his dashboard and
tires. When he finishes, he burns out of the car wash, leaving a trail
of armorall on the asphalt.*
*It's a beautiful day, he thinks to himself as he bounces down
Central Avenue. He picks up his cellular phone and calls Auntie to
make sure everything is alright.*
"Auntie, you alright?"
"Yeah Nephew, everything is good. We killing them as
usual."
"How much work do we have left?"
"We have enough to last us until tomorrow," Auntie
replies.
"Cool, I'll be by there a little later."
"Alright, later Nephew!"
*Tony's crew is on point. He doesn't have to be around there,
because everyone knows their position. The only reason he hangs
around there is so no one will think he's afraid to be on front line
with them. He wants them to always recognize that he's right there*

with them regardless of what.

Beep! Beep! *Tony hits the horn as he pulls up to E's house. E runs down the stairs. As E approaches the car Tony slides over to the passenger seat.*

"Drive!" Tony shouts. *E gets in, shakes Tony's hand and takes off.*

As they're riding E turns to Tony and says, **"this motherfucker ride good as hell. What year is it?"**

"What year are we in?" Tony asks arrogantly.

"Yeah?"

"Syke nah, I'm just bullshitting," Tony admits. "This is only an 88." *Tony is lying through his teeth. E won't be able to tell if it's an 88 or not because the body shape doesn't change much on Porsches.*

"Only an 88, listen to you like that's a long time ago," E replies.

"Shit, it is. That was almost two years ago."

Tony has never told any one he bought the car from the auction, not even his boys. His motto is if they want to believe he bought the car brand new off the lot, then let them think that.

"How much did you pay for this?"

"$46,000," Tony lies.

"Got damn, you could have paid for all four years of college with $46,000. What's up with that college shit any way? Are you still going?"

Tony hesitates before he answers.

"Yeah."

"Damn nigga, you don't sound too sure about that. You took a long time to answer."

"I'm sure, I just want to save up some more money so I can be straight." *Tony is babbling. Actually he stopped thinking about college some time ago. The fast money is starting to blurry his vision. It seems like the more money he makes the more he wants to make.*

"Did you go to the skating rink, last night?" E asks.

"Oh yeah, let me tell you. I met a bad motherfucker last night."

"Where, in the rink?" E asks.

"No, after the rink. Check, I'm coming down the Parkway doing a hundred and some change. I wasn't bullshitting. I'm dipping in and out of traffic. Every time I dip, the car behind me dips. They were high beaming all the way down the Parkway, but I didn't stop though. When I got off at the South Orange Ave. exit they got off right with me. The car pulled up on the side of me. It was a gold Honda Accord with four bad bitches in there. They all were smiling and waving, so I waved back. Then the passenger calls out my name. I didn't know this broad from a can of paint. She jumped out and gave me her number. Yo, this little motherfucker was bad as hell, E. I suppose to hook up with her later on tonight."

"How did she know your name?"

"I don't know," Tony replies. I kept asking her where she knew me from, but she wouldn't tell me."

"You know how shit is," says E.

"Yeah, the streets are talking," Tony adds.

"Shit, if I was riding like this I would be fucking all day everyday," says E.

"See, that's where we different, it's money over chicks for me. I mean pussy alright, but I'd rather have that cash," Tony explains.

"Man, keep mines balanced. I want a lot of money, and a lot of pussy!" E shouts. *They both laugh.*

"E, you're crazy."

"Yo, the reason I called you over is to let you know we are almost ready to re-up. I'm waiting for JJ to get the rest of the money to me. I just wanted to make sure you were still going to hook us up with your connect."

"Alright, cool. I told you whenever ya'll ready. Your man JJ, he holds everything down, huh?" Tony asks.

"Yeah, we don't have to do nothing. I had him around

me for a while now. I raised him good, he don't steal or
nothing, I taught him a long time ago that this game is based on
loyalty and trust.

"That's right," Tony agrees. "So you let him bag up and
everything?"

"Nah, we bag it up and drop it off to him," E explains.

"Ok," says Tony. "Jump on the Parkway; I want to
show you something." *E turns onto the Parkway.*

"So how much do you make out there on your block?"
Tony asks.

"Our block is not rocking like yours," E admits. "We
only make about 1,500 a day; it's too many motherfuckers out
there."

"You have to start eliminating motherfuckers," Tony
suggests.

"It's alright though, because we cut the coke. So even if
it takes a long time to finish we still make a nice profit."

"Cut, what kind of cut?" Tony asks.

"Lactose," E replies.

"That's why shit is so slow, ya'll selling bullshit," says
Tony. That's why my block is rocking like that. The same way
I get it, the same way I put it on the block. That's why niggas
can't compete with me."

"Do you make a big profit like that?" E asks.

"It don't matter as long as I make more than I started
with, I'm cool. I'm just keeping my customers happy. When
they spend, they make me happy. Don't be greedy, and try to
make all the money today. Try to make a little money everyday,
forever. Remember, longevity, that's the name of this game,"
Tony explains.

"Longevity, huh?"

"Yo, get off at the next exit," Tony instructs. "Make a
right at the corner, my house is the last one on the right."

*The rest of the day E keeps thinking longevity. What Tony
said made a lot of sense. E can't understand how he has more time*

in the game than Tony, but Tony seems to be much more advanced than him.

Tony seems to be much more advanced because he had time to observe. Just like a basketball player, who rides the bench. Game after game he watches the players on the court. Finally the coach puts him in the game, and to everyone's surprise he turns out to be a MVP, all because he studied from the sideline. He knew what to do, and what not to do. He learned from the other player's mistakes. While E and Du were already on the street, Tony was watching from the bench.

CHAPTER 24

Later that day

    Tony picked up the girl he met the night before. They spend a few hours riding around town listening to slow music.
    "As soon as my people call me we're off to the movies, alright?" Tony asks.
    "Alright," Andrea replies.
    Tony has been observing her. He can tell she's used to being around big timers. He can tell by the way she carries herself. From the way she walks, talks, and even how she plays the passenger seat. She's laid back with her Anne Klein shades on, windows rolled up, just looking straight ahead. Almost, like the world outside the car doesn't exist. No matter how many people stare as they ride by, she acts as if though she doesn't notice them. It's like she has seen it all, because nothing seems to impress her.
    Tony looks her from head to toe, over and over. She's beautiful. She's definitely wife material. He knows he has to make a good impression on her, because he doesn't want to blow his chances of being with her.
    "What movie theater are we going to?" Andrea asks.
    "Which one do you want to go to?"
    "Not Perth Amboy, him and his boys go out there from time to time, when they're in town.
    He, means her boyfriend. She told Tony she had a boyfriend but it wasn't working out because he didn't have time for her. He's some big time cat, as she describes him. He mostly works out of town. He sells kilos at a time. He works from Maryland on down to the Carolinas. Sometimes he's away from home for months. When he comes home, he gives her a couple of thousand, and he's back on the road.

Ring, ring!

"Hello," says Tony.

"Nephew, come through."

This is Auntie. She's calling to tell him they're finish with the last package.

"Alright, give me twenty minutes." CLICK! "That was them. I'm going to ride over there and then we're out."

"Alright baby," Andrea replies.

Andrea doesn't talk much. Tony can tell she has a lot on her mind. He's not sure if she's stressing over her boyfriend, or she's digging his style. Why wouldn't she be attracted to Tony? He's a slick handsome brother, and on top of that, the word on the street is he has an asshole full of money.

Tony pulls to the block and runs in. He runs right back out with a brown shopping bag. When he gets back in the car he notices panties wrapped around his rear view mirror. He automatically looks over at Andrea as he's pulling off. To his surprise, she's sitting there fully exposed. Her skirt is on the floor. He doesn't know what to say. He just stares at her thick thighs, and her hairy pussy.

"I'm not in the mood for a movie. I'm horny as hell, I haven't been fucked in six months," Andrea claims.

Six months, got damn, Tony thinks to himself. Before he can speak she reaches over and grabs his dick. She starts sucking him off. Tony can barely drive as she teases him with her tongue.

"Chill, chill, put your skirt on," says Tony, *as they pull up to his apartment.*

She doesn't want to stop. She continues to suck until he snatches her head off him.

"Come on; let's go in," Tony instructs.

Tony grabs the bag of money and proceeds up the stairs. Andrea walks up the stairs first. Being that she doesn't have any panties on, Tony can see her entire ass under the tiny skirt.

When they enter the apartment, Tony takes the money out of the bag and lays it on the table. In total it's $15,000. There's no *reason to lay the money on the table. That's his way of showing off as he counts the money out loud. When he turns around, Andrea is stretched out on the bed ass naked, with two fingers in her pussy. She's finger fucking herself. What has come over her, he asks himself. He had no clue that she was like that. He thought she was a good girl.*

"Tony, I have three holes, fuck all of them! Please," she begs, *as she fingers herself. Tony walks over to the bed and does as she said. She sucks and fucks Tony all night long. She puts him to sleep just like a newborn baby.*

At three thirty am, she wakes Tony.

"Baby, I need to use your phone, they're beeping me from my house using 911."

Tony, hands her the phone. He's still half sleep.

Andrea starts dialing.

"Hello, Ma? No!" she screams. "Is he all right?" she asks. "I'll be right there."

She hangs up and passes Tony the phone.

"It's my boyfriend. He got shot."

"Where? Was he out of town?"

"No," Andrea replies. "He was down on Irvine Turner Boulevard."

"Is he all right?"

"I don't know. They shot him 14 times. They don't know if he is going to make it. I have to go to the hospital, call me a cab."

She hurries to the door. "Baby, I'll call you as soon as I can," she shouts, as she walks to the porch. Tony watches her from his window, until the cab arrives.

He forgot to put the money up, due to the stunt Andrea pulled. He places the bag of money inside the clothes hamper then he dozes off.

At 4:45am Tony is awakened by a car alarm. He peeks out the window. He surprisingly sees his lights flashing. Somebody is trying to steal my car, he thinks out loud.

He runs out, not realizing he only has his boxers on. When he gets to the car he sees no car thieves. He turns off the alarm, and walks around the car examining it. When he gets to the passenger side, he sees a shadow behind him. Before he could move, SMACK! It feels like someone has hit him in the head with a hammer. He's so dizzy. He tries to shake it off, but then comes another one. SMACK! This one hit him right on his forehead, on top of his right eye. He falls to the ground. He can't see out of his right eye. Blood is everywhere. He grabs hold to the bumper trying to pull himself up, when SMACK! This one lands on the top of his head. The lights go out.

CHAPTER 25

Meanwhile, E is driving JJ home. They've been on the block all night.

"I'm tired as hell," says E. "I thought we were never going to finish."

"Yeah, those last ones took forever to sell," says JJ.

"The reason I wanted to stay out is so we can hurry up and finish. I have some new plans I want to try out."

"You know I'm with you, in whatever you're trying to do," JJ replies.

"Trust me, I already know, you don't have to tell me that. Ever since I first met you, I saw something different in you. That's what attracted me to you. You're not like the rest of these niggas; you listen. That's what the old heads taught me. You have to listen in order to learn. I know I'm not much older than you, but you're like a little brother to me. I got mad love for you."

"I got love for you too," JJ replies. "I wanna let you know that I would never cross you for nothing in this world. You're the only nigga that ever showed me love. When we're out there on the block, it feels good to know that someone has my back."

"Well, I'm glad you know that I got your back. Even before we started doing business together, we were friends. So after all this is over, I hope we can still be friends."

"No doubt," JJ agrees.

E pulls over, parks and turns off the lights.

"Never look at it like you work for me. Look at it like business. Do your job, get your money and take care of

JJ. Anytime you start wondering, how much money the next motherfucker is making, you got problems."

"I never looked at it like that."

"Nah, I'm just telling you. Another thing, I'm never going to hold you down. Use me as a stepping-stone. Get your money up, and do you. If not, you'll be running in place for the rest of your life. Do you hear me?" E asks.

"Yeah, I hear you."

"Well, I'm about to pull out. I'll hit you in the afternoon when I'm ready. I love you!"

JJ gets out and slams the door. "I love you too!"

E pulls off, and goes to Kless Diner to get breakfast.

E has genuine love for JJ. He also feels sympathy for him. JJ has had it rough his entire life. He's only nineteen years old and he has been on his own for five years already. His father died from AIDS when his was ten years old. Then four years later he watched his mother die slowly from the same disease, leaving him and his ten year old brother by themselves.

His father was a skin-popping junkie, who had several extramarital affairs. His mother on the other hand, was a good clean religious woman. She was a Jehovah's Witness. She contracted the virus from JJ's father. She spent her entire life preaching the word all the way to her last day.

After she passed away JJ's brother was placed in a foster home, but JJ refused to go to a home. Every time they placed him somewhere, he would run away. Before he hooked up with E, he was sleeping wherever he could. Most of the time he would pay crack heads two or three bottles and they would let him stay in their houses at night. He hardly ever ate home cooked meals. The majority of his meals came from the Chinese store. Chicken and French fries on Monday, Beef fried rice on Tuesdays and so forth. On Fridays he would treat himself to a Seafood combination; that's shrimp, scallops, and crabmeat over yellow rice.

E made a promise to himself and JJ that when he makes it to the top he will bring JJ with him. JJ's dream is to become a famous rapper. He spends all of his spare time writing rhymes in his notepad. He wants to make it big, so one day he can get custody of his little brother. E told him that once he blows up, he's going to start a record label and let him have full control over it.

CHAPTER 26

When Tony awakens his vision is blurry. He's sitting against the wall. He looks down at his hands, they're tied together with rope, and so are his ankles. He also has tape over his mouth. His boxers are covered with blood. He can't quite remember what happened. He doesn't realize what's going on until he sees two masked men running around his apartment, looking through everything. He can't see out of his right eye, it's swollen shut.

The masked men are running from room to room, opening closets, and looking under the bed and inside the cushions of the sofa. The taller of the two men walk over to him, and kicks him in the chest.

"Where the fuck is the money?" the taller man asks. *Tony can't speak. He's shaking his head no.*

"The motherfucker said it's in here for sure!" shouts the shorter man. *The short man then walks over to Tony and smacks him in the face with the gun.* **"Where the fuck is the money? If you don't tell me where the money is, I'm going to shoot you in your motherfucking head."**

Tony watches them tear everything up. They're going through all of his personal belongings. He's going through a bunch of emotions. He's scared for his life. He knows they're going to kill him, but he doesn't know when. He also feels helpless, what is he supposed to do just sit there and wait for them to kill him or should he make a run for the door. Most of all he feels violated.

"Do you want me to bring the motherfucker in?" the short man asks the tall man.

"Yeah," the tall man replies.

Tony sits there clueless; he wonders know who they're

talking about. The short man walks out the door, while the tall man walks over to Tony and begins pistol-whipping him. Tony can't scream. He just grunts as the butt of the gun crashes into his skull. It feels like some one is dropping cinder blocks on top of his head. Blood is everywhere.

Tony hears the front door open. He hears two sets of footsteps. When he peeks up he sees the short man dragging some one by the collar.

"Please, don't let him see me," *whispers the voice.*

"Bitch, shut up!" *the short man shouts.* **"Where is the money? We looked all over ain't no money in here."**

The man finally drags the person into the bedroom. Tony has to look twice. It's Andrea.

"I swear he had $15,000 in here. It was right there on the table when I left," *Andrea whispers.*

Tony doesn't know what's going on. Did they snatch her out of the cab, he asks himself? He's so confused.

Smack! *The tall man slaps Andrea.*

"If we don't find the money, I'm going to kill both of you motherfuckers in here!"

"I swear to God it was in here!" *Andrea screams. She cries loud and hard. You can see fear all over her face. Tony is not sure what he should do. Maybe if he gives them the money they will leave. Maybe not, he thinks. They may still kill them.*

"Umm, Umm," *he utters to catch their attention.*

"What?" *asks the tall man.* **"Are you trying to say something?"**

Tony nods his head yes. The tall man runs over and snatches the tape off of his mouth.

"The money is in the hamper," *Tony whispers.* **Look in the dirty clothes hamper. I got 15,000 in there. Please don't kill her, she ain't got nothing to do with this."**

The short man runs over to the hamper, while the tall man puts the tape back on Tony's mouth. Andrea stands there watching. Never has she looked Tony in the eyes. He just wants to make eye contact with her so he can get a sense of what's happening. He feels so sorry for her. He thinks it's his fault she got caught up in the mix of this.

"I got it!" says the short man, *as he counts the 15 stacks.* **"She was right!"**

"I told you," Andrea replies.

They all gather in a huddle whispering. Tony can't make out what the men are saying, but he can't believe what he thinks he hears Andrea whispering.

"Kill him. Ya'll gotta kill him. I can't be walking around like that. He knows my face. Please kill him. If you don't kill him, he'll kill me, please," she begs.

Oh shit, Tony thinks to himself. It was all a set up. She's with them. All the fucking meant nothing, it was only business. Tony has been played for a piece of pussy.

The short man walks toward Tony with his gun in his hand. Tony realizes it's over. He closes his eyes. They're about to kill him like Andrea begged them to. **Boom! Boom! Boom!**

Tony peeks out of one eye wondering why he didn't feel the shots. To his surprise Andrea is laid out on the floor, squirming around with blood dripping from the side of her mouth.

Boom! Boom! *The man stands over her and fires two more shots. That's it. Andrea lays there motionless. Her eyes roll up in her head, she's dead. After he kicks her to make sure, they both take off leaving the door wide open.*

CHAPTER 27

E and Du have been calling Tony all morning. They finally decide to ride through his block. It's not like him to ignore phone calls.

When they get to Auntie's house they see that the block is empty. Auntie is sitting on the porch.

"Auntie, is Tony in there?" Du asks.

"No, that's who I'm waiting for. I haven't heard from him all day. He won't pick up his phone. The block is dry, nobody ain't got shit. Do you have anything?"

"Nah," Du replies. Maybe he's handling something, I'll see if I can find him."

"Tell him to hurry up, shit coming!" she shouts, *as they pull off.*

"Let's ride by his apartment; maybe he's in there. He was supposed to take some girl out last night; he's probably still laid up with her."

E gets on the Parkway and follows the same instructions Tony gave him. When they turn onto the block, two detectives, who are standing in the middle of the street, stop them.

"You can't drive through here, son." As they look further they see three unmarked police cars, and a bunch of Newark cop cars lined up and down the block. E makes a u- turn and parks around the corner. As they jog down the block they notice a group of people crowded around Tony's house.

"Oh shit, they're at Tony's house!" E shouts.

"What the fuck happened?" asks Du? When they finally get close enough, they see yellow tape all around the house. The police photographer is in the hallway taking pictures. All the doors are

wide open.

"Yeah, they're in Tony's apartment," says E.

"Damn, Tony!" Du shouts.

Seconds later the coroners come walking out carrying a body bag. The boys almost lose their minds. They try to run over and find out what's happening, but the police officers push them away. The coroners struggle to get the body inside the van. Once they finally dump the bag inside and slam the doors, Du almost faints. They both stand there holding each other up as the van pulls off.

They see a woman walking out with the detectives. It's Tony's mother. They run over to her. Du hugs her.

"Ma, what happened?" Du asks. Mom's eyes are swollen from crying.

"I don't know. That's what we're trying to figure out. I didn't even know about this apartment," Mom says sarcastically. "They contacted me from his license. They got the address and came to the house. He's alright though. They took him downtown for questioning." Both boys exhale, hoping they heard her right.

"Did you say, he's alright?" E asks.

"Yes," Mom replies.

"So who was that in the coroners van?" Du asks.

"Oh, that wasn't Tony, thank God," Mom replies. "That was some young girl. They found her in the apartment dead. She was shot five times. It's a mess in there, there's blood everywhere."

"Did Tony get shot?" Du asks.

"No, when the police arrived he was in there tied up with tape covering his mouth. They beat him bad. I told him over and over to leave these streets alone. He didn't listen. If he gets out of this, I bet he'll listen now. All of you need to leave the streets alone. It's ya'll fault, he ain't doing nothing but following ya'll." They both stand there just listening. Little does she know Tony is further in the game than both of them.

E and Du are baffled. They can't imagine who would do this to Tony.

"Boys, I'm leaving. I'm going downtown to the precinct to see what's going on."

"Do you want us to go with you?" Du questions.

"No, I'm going by myself. I'll call you after I talk to him."

They get in their separate cars and pull off. Mom goes to the precinct, and the boys just drive around with no destination, in total suspense.

CHAPTER 28

The police held Tony for two days. They questioned him over and over about the murder. Never did he tell them that the girl set him up, because if he told that he would have to tell about the money, and that would open other doors.

Besides, Tony isn't a snitch. He knows he has to play by the rules of the game that he chose to play. With fast money comes murder Tony is well aware of that.

He made up some lie about a jealous boyfriend. He told them she mentioned she had a jealous boyfriend who always followed her around. At first they didn't believe his story but they had to go with it. It was impossible for him to tie his own self up like that, and his fingerprints didn't match with the ones all over the house.

Du walks in Tony's room. He's upset at the sight of Tony's face. Both eyes are swollen shut, and blackened. His mouth is also swollen. He has a white bandage wrapped around his head.

E walks in seconds behind Du.

"What's up?" Tony shouts. He's trying to act as normal as he can. Neither one of them respond, they're just staring at him. "I look fucked up right?"

"You here though, that's most important," says Du. E doesn't know what to say; this is too much for him.

"Do you know who did it?" Du asks.

"No, but I know it was a set up. The bitch that got killed, she was in on the whole thing."

"Get the fuck out of here! How you know?" E questions.

"Me and the bitch was fucking all night. I fell asleep. In the middle of the night she wakes me up with some bullshit about

her boy friend getting shot up, so she leaves. One hour later my car alarm goes off. I run out there, and these motherfuckers are out there waiting for me. I would have never known it was her, if they wouldn't have brought her back in. They brought her back because they couldn't find the money. Yo, this bitch begged them niggas to kill me. She was a cold-hearted bitch. She kept begging, kill him, please kill him. She thought I would see her somewhere later, but instead of killing me they killed her."

"Why do you think they killed her?" E asks.

"They probably thought she would tell someone," Tony replies.

"Who were they?" Du asks.

"I don't know they had on masks."

"Did they get you for a lot?" E asks.

"Only 15 grand, I can't get over that girl she seemed so innocent. I wonder how many other niggas she did that to."

"Word up," E agrees.

"Somebody had to put her on me, because the night I met her she already knew my name."

"Yeah, that was a set up," E agrees.

"So, are you going to lay low for a while?" Du asks.

"Lay low for what? I'm going to do what I been doing, get money. I just lost $15,000, I have to get that back.

At this point they realize Tony is no longer the schoolboy they know and love. Tony is officially turned out.

"Tony, you need to slow down, at least until you find out where the set up came from," Du suggests.

"For real Tony," E agrees.

"I know your mother is worried to death," says Du.

"Yeah, don't put her through this," E adds.

"I don't want to stress Mom Dukes out but I gotta eat. My block is bringing in about $15,000 a day now. That's all they got me for was one days worth of work. I'll get that back tomorrow, dumb, broke ass niggas. If I find out who did it, I swear to God on my life, I'm going to kill them!"

Nothing they're saying makes sense to Tony. The fast money has taken full control of his life. His addiction for fast money is bigger than the addiction the crack heads have for the cocaine.

CHAPTER 29

The next morning

    Tony is ready to rock and roll. The house robbery means nothing to him. Instead of slowing down, he plans to step it up.

    Right now, him and Flaco are in Flaco's apartment. Tony no longer meets Flaco on the street. It's too much money being exchanged to make the transaction on the street. Tony feels good to know Flaco trusts him enough to bring him to his house.

    "Tony, what's up? I'm sorry to hear what happened to you. You have to be careful in this game. You can't trust anyone. When things like this happen, 90% of the time it's someone close to you. It has to be somebody in your circle. Tony, always remember, it's not the person on the outside you have to worry about, because he knows nothing. You have to worry about the one on the inside. He knows everything, your moves, your likes, your dislikes, and your fears. Tony don't ever forget that."

    What Flaco just said adds more fuel to the fire. Ever since that night Tony has been trying to figure out who could have set him up. All kinds of crazy thoughts have been running through his head. He even thought about his boys Du and E, maybe it was Auntie. He doesn't know but it stays on his mind all day and all night.

    "So Flaco, what you got?"

    "Beautiful Tony," Flaco replies. "The material is beautiful. I just got them in this morning. Here look," he says, as he hands the brick to him. It's not even opened yet; the wrapper is still on it. Tony cuts through the tape with the steak knife. Then he wipes the grease off with a paper towel. Finally he cuts the rubber casing off.

    Just like Flaco said it's beautiful, white as snow. It still has the stamp imprinted on top. The stamp is an eagle imprint. All Flaco's kilos have the same stamp on them. That's a way of knowing what cartel they come from. Flaco has taught Tony all about cocaine. He can now spot garbage cocaine a mile away.

Tony breaks off a corner of the brick. The inside is full of bright, shiny scales. This is what you call fish scale cocaine.

"Yeah, this shit raw," says Tony, as he lays the corner of the brick down. Hachew! Hachew! Tony sneezes. The loud smell of the cocaine fills the room causing Tony to sneeze. The smell is similar to fingernail polish. If you stand over it too long it will give you a headache.

Tony hands Flaco the bag of money. Inside the bag is $31,500. $21,000 is his and $10,500 belongs to E & Du. He's buying a kilo for himself, and a half a kilo for E and Du.

"Thirty-one, five right?" Flaco asks.

"Yeah, count it," Tony suggests.

"Poppy I trust you. You say it's thirty-one, five then I know it's there."

Flaco never counts the money when Tony gives it to him. Flaco said that's total disrespect, and if he didn't trust him, he wouldn't do business with him. So in exchange Tony never weighs the coke Flaco gives him. That's to show him he has the same trust for him.

Tony packs the work inside a shopping bag and sprays air freshener inside the bag. That's to hold down the aroma of the cocaine.

"Alright Flaco."

"Ok be safe Poppy. Call me when you reach your destination."

Tony has to hurry, the block is dry. He also has to meet Du and E to give them their half a bird.

He dashes out and jumps in E's jeep. E let him borrow it. Tony put the Porsche up ever since the robbery. He doesn't feel comfortable driving it because he feels marked. Especially since he doesn't know who did it. He can be looking right at him and he still wouldn't know it.

CHAPTER 30

It's 6:00 PM, and Tony is just getting the work on the block. This is his first time on the block since the house robbery. Every one has heard about it, so they all look at him strangely. They don't know what to say to him. He plans to keep his distance, because he doesn't want anyone questioning him about it. Tony's worst fear is them thinking he's soft because of what happened. He's scared they will no longer respect him. He's waiting for any little thing to happen so he can take it to the extreme, just to show them nothing has changed. He wants them to know he's still the same guy they have grown to fear. He got caught slipping; it could happen to anyone.

Tony stands on the porch for hours, just observing. He's trying to figure out which one of these guys could have set him up. Was it a member of his team? Or a member of the other crews out there? Everybody is acting strange, so it's hard to tell.

RING! RING! *Tony hears the phone in the apartment ringing. Tony runs in to answer it.*

"Hello? Hello?"

"HELLO! You have a collect call from Trenton State Prison, caller please state your name," says the operator.

"Kareem!" shouts the voice. "Do you accept?" the operator asks.

"Yes," Tony replies. "Reemie, what's up?"

"Who is this?" Reemie asks.

"This Tony, motherfucker!"

"What's up, Cuzzo? Long time no hear from," says Reemie.

"Yeah, I know I've been real busy," Tony explains.

"I been trying to get in touch with you," says Reemie.
"I been hearing big things about you. You're holding it down,
huh?"

"I'm doing all right," Tony replies modestly.

"Where's my mother?" Reemie asks.

"She left out for a minute."

"What's up with her? Is she all right?"

"Yeah," Tony answers hesitantly. *Tony can't tell Reemie
his mother is a crack head. Reemie doesn't know. When he went
away to prison his mother was a beautiful, working class woman.
He rather let Reemie find out for himself.*

"I heard about that bullshit that happened to you,"
Reemie says.

"What bullshit?"

"That house shit," Reemie replies.
How does he know about that, Tony asks himself.

"How did you find out about that?"

"The news gets down to prison faster than you think,"
says Reemie. "Everyone was talking about it but I didn't know
it was you. I never heard of no motherfucking Nephew."

"So how did you find out it was me?"

"That's what I called to tell you," Reemie admits. "I
know who did that to you."

Tony's heart starts pounding. "Wh, who?" he stutters.

"Hold up, check it out, the other morning I called my
man up, and he started babbling about a vick (robbery) he had
done, and how he came off with 15 g's. That's how much they
got you for, right?"

"Yeah," Tony replies. "Who is he?"

"Hold up. He mentioned Tony, so I didn't say anything,
I kept listening. So I asked him how you looked. He described
you to the fullest. He knew everything about you, the Porsche,
where your mother lived and everything. Some other nigga put
him on you. They used the bitch to reel you in. That's how they
work. They got a squad of bad, model looking chicks that they

117

use just to set niggas up."

"Who the fuck is he?" Tony asks impatiently.

"Harry James," Reemie replies. "In the joint we called him Buck-Wild. Me and this nigga did three years in Trenton together. We're tight as hell, like brothers."

"Is he just coming home?"

"Nah, he's been home for almost a year now," Reemie replies.

"Did you tell him we were cousins?"

"Hell no, I didn't tell him shit!" Reemie shouts. "Ever since he came home, he's been taking care of me. Money in my account, boots, food packages, everything."

"So who was the other nigga?" Tony asks.

"Most likely it was Smitty. That's the only nigga he fucks with like that. Was he tall and skinny?"

"Yeah."

"That was Smitty."

"Where are they at now?" Tony asks.

"Right now they laying low. I haven't been able to get in touch with him, but he knows I'm about to come home so he will be sure to be somewhere so I can find him."

"When are you coming home?"

"No longer than two weeks. I maxxed out already."
(Maxxed out means he did all the time he can do for the crime he committed.)

"That's alright."

"We'll deal with Buck-Wild when I check in. It will be easy because he trust me. I don't want to talk too much on this phone. I don't trust it."

"Me either," Tony agrees.

"Be careful," Reemie warns. "Watch your back, he's serious. He ain't to be played with, so don't take him lightly. It's a wonder you still here, normally he don't work like that. All his robberies end with a homicide. Be thankful. Don't do anything until I get home, just lay low."

"Alright, I won't do anything."
"Alright Cuzzo, I'll catch you in two weeks!"
"Peace!" Tony shouts. Click!

After they hang up Tony debates about telling his boys. He isn't sure because he doesn't want the word to spread all over the street. It's not that he thinks they would deliberately cross him, but then again he doesn't trust anyone right now. Tony realizes he has to do something.

He spends the rest of the night thinking about how he's going to handle Buck-Wild.

CHAPTER 31

For the last couple of days, Tony has been playing it cool. He hasn't been coming around much, unless Auntie needed him to drop off work. He hasn't been staying at his mother's house either. He remembers Reemie telling him, they knew where she lived and he doesn't want to bring any trouble there. He's been staying in different hotels every night.

It is 12, in the afternoon. Tony is driving with no destination. He's tired. He barely sleeps at night. All night long, he visions Andrea lying on the floor dead. He jumps in his sleep and wakes up sweaty with his heart racing.

He dials Du's phone. Du picks up. Tony tells them to meet him at John's Place for lunch.

When Tony gets there, he sees them in the truck. They don't recognize him though, in his new vehicle. He has a Dodge caravan with limo-tinted windows.

He pulls on the side of them, as they're peeking he jumps out. They get out right after. When they look in his face, they notice he doesn't look like himself. His eyes are baggy from no sleep, and he doesn't have a haircut or a shave. His shorts are wrinkled and his t-shirt is on backwards.

"Damn! Tony what the fuck happened to you? You look fucked up," says Du.

"Got damn," E agrees.

"Not right now," he whispers, *as he opens the door for them.*

While they're at the table eating, Tony decides to tell them, who it was that robbed him.

"Tony, what's up?" E asks. "You acting crazy as hell."

"I wasn't going to tell nobody this, but I know who robbed me!"

"Who?" Du asks.

"Do ya'll know a joker name Buck-Wild, Harry James?" *They both sit there, with their eyes stretched wide opened. They respond seconds later.*

"Yeah," Du replies. "Was it him?

"Do you know him?" Tony asks.

"We know of him?" Du replies.

"What do you know of him?"

"I know he plays for keeps."

"I heard," Tony admits. "Where is he from?"

"All over. He tried to car jack us before; he shot the whole car up."

"Yeah?" Tony questions.

"I promised to never repeat this again, but I watched him kill my weed connect, broad daylight on Sixteenth Ave," E confesses.

"How does he know you?" Du asks.

"I don't know that yet, but I will know in a couple of weeks."

They all sit quietly. Nobody has much of an appetite anymore. Both E and Du know Buck-Wild is a tough match to go up against, but he has violated their best friend.

"So what are we going to do?" E asks, *hoping that Tony will say nothing and let it pass, but to his surprise Tony says,* "He has to be dealt with. He violated me. I don't give a fuck who he is and what he has done. He's a regular man, and he bleeds the same way we bleed. If he can be seen, he can be touched. He should have killed me when he had me. The worst thing he could do, was let me live. I will have no mercy on him. Word is bond, he should have killed me like that bitch begged him to do!"

They have never seen this cold and fearless look in Tony eyes before.

"What time is it?" Tony asks.

"10 o'clock," Du replies.

"Damn, I have to meet somebody in twenty minutes. Follow me, I want ya'll to come with me."

They jump in their car and follow Tony. When they reach Stratford Place, Tony gets out and gestures for them to follow him.

They walk through the alleyway of the apartment building. Tony rings the bell to the basement apartment. An old man answers. He tells Tony to come in and have a seat.

As they're sitting in the living room, another man walks out carrying a big black duffle bag.

"What's up?" *he says, as he enters the room.*

Tony gets up and says, "What up Country?" *and shakes his hand. E and Du, are just sitting there observing.* "What you got?"

"A little of everything," Country claims, *while unzipping the bag. Country reaches in the bag, and pulls out a snub nose revolver.*

"What's that?" Tony asks.

"A snub nose 38."

"That's too small, we need some big shit."

Country starts pulling all his guns out, one by one. In total he has twelve. He has 2-tech nines, 1-uzi, 3- nine-millies, 2- four fives, 1- three eighty, a forty-four magnum, the snub nose 38, and an M-16 military assault rifle.

Tony gestures for his boys to come over to the table, as he picks up every gun, one by one, aiming them at the wall. He peeks out of one eye, looking down the nose of each gun.

"Which one you getting?" E asks.

"Which ones do you think we should get?"

"I want the .44 magnum," Du replies.

"I like the .45 and the tech and the...fuck it I like them all," says E.

"Well let's get them all," says Tony.

"Stop playing, we don't need all them guns," Du replies.

"That's too many guns."

"Yeah, and we getting too much money," says Tony.

"You can never have too many guns," Country claims.

"How much for the whole bag?" Tony asks.

"The whole bag?" *Country stares at the guns while calculating out loud.* "If I sell them, piece-by-piece, I'll get about $7,500."

"Well, we're not talking about piece by piece. We want the whole bag, what's up?" Tony asks.

"Give me $6,200, and take the whole bag."

"Is that the best you can do?"

"And I'll throw in three bulletproof vests."

"Bet," says Tony. "How much cash ya'll got on you?"

"I got $1,200," says Du.

"I got $1,700," says E.

"I got $2,300. How much is that all together?"

"$5,200," Du says.

"Here, Country, take the $5,200 and come over to my block later, and pick up the other thousand."

"All right," Country replies.

Country lets them out the door. E goes out first, to open up the hatch of the jeep. Then Tony and Du walk out struggling with the bag. They dump the bag in the back and pull off.

They take the guns to JJ's house. That's where they'll stash them.

Ever since the fellas found out about Buck-Wild they have been inseparable. They're together all day everyday. Now they all carry guns on their waist all the time. This is nothing new to Tony he has been doing this ever since the boys jacked him up in the hallway, but them two never held guns in their hands before. This is something big to them. Their attitudes have changed drastically. They're acting so cocky. If someone even looks at them wrong they're ready to draw their guns. They made a pact that wherever they see Buck-Wild, they're going to finish him right there.

CHAPTER 32

---

*Tony is riding down Market St. He has to meet Reemie;
he's coming home today. As Tony approaches Broad St. he starts
slowing down to see if he spots him. Maybe he'll spot me first, Tony
thinks to himself. Tony told him he would be in the Porsche.*

*Tony has not driven the car in two weeks. The only reason
he brought it out today is to show Reemie he's not bullshitting out
here.*

*Tony is looking all over for Reemie but he doesn't see him
anywhere. Tony watches as a man walks out of the arcade. He's
tall and wide. This can't be Reemie, Tony thinks to himself. The
last time Tony saw his cousin he was a little skinny boy. This has
to be him. He's wearing state clothes. He has on state boots, beige
khakis, beige state coat and a beige wool hat on his head. He has a
full beard. This guy is huge.*

*He walks to the corner and looks around. When he spots
Tony's car he squints to see if it's him. He throws his arms up in the
air. Tony smiles at him and Reemie runs to the car. Everyone at the
bus stop stares as the big gorilla runs across the street. Ten years,
Tony thinks. Reemie looks totally different. Had it not been for the
birthmark on Reemie's face he wouldn't have recognized him. Tony
was only nine years old the last time he saw Reemie.*

"Cuzzo!" Reemie shouts, *as he gets closer to the car.
Tony jumps out to hug him. He can't get his arms around him.
Reemie is 6 feet 2 inches and weighs a solid 240 pounds; all
muscle. Tony only stands 5 feet 8 inches, and weighs a mere 135
pounds.*

"Cuzzo, what's up baby?" Reemie asks.

"Ten motherfucking years!" Tony shouts. *They*

stand there looking each other up and down. **You look like a motherfucking giant," says Tony. "You're wide as hell."**

"Shit, you would be wide as hell too if all you did was work out all motherfucking day. It seems like I did the whole ten years on the pull up bar." *Reemie starts laughing as he squeezes into the tiny little car.* **"Damn, little Tony pushing a Porsche. You must be living it up."**

"I'm doing alright," Tony says modestly. *Tony hates to be praised.*

"All right? Nigga please, your name is ringing in the prison system. Nephew this, Nephew that, Nephew bought a Porsche $50,000 cash money. Nephew shot Slick Rick. Nephew banging two pies a week on his block. That's all I been hearing. Come to find out Nephew is your little punk ass," he says sarcastically.

"Niggas knew about me popping Rick?"

"Yeah, Rick was extorting a lot of motherfuckers. Where is he at now?"

"I heard he's in Rahway Prison," Tony replies.

"He's a bitch ass nigga in the joint, can't fight a bit. Me and him did two years in Annandale together. But on the street he's a monster," Reemie admits. "He fuck with them guns real heavy, he'll blast your ass in a second. But you set his ass straight."

"Go ahead," Tony says humbly. "You were down Annandale too?"

"Yeah, I started out down Jamesburg, then Annandale, then Bordentown, and then they shipped me to Rahway. I did my last four years in Trenton."

"Shit, they shipped your ass all over."

"Yeah, altogether I stayed in lock up about three years of my bid. I was a wild young nigga until I got to Trenton with them old heads, they wasn't having that dumb shit."

They park on Halsey St. As they walk around the corner to Dr. Jays everyone peeks at Reemie, they're scared to let him see them staring.

"Let me get you out of that state bullshit you got on."

Once they get upstairs, Tony picks up all kinds of things for Reemie. Reemie has been gone for 10 years. He doesn't know anything about the latest styles. When he left dudes were wearing Swedish knits, and tight ass dress shirts.

At the register Aisha starts to ring everything up. **"What's up, Aisha?"**

"Hey Tony, how are you?"

"Who is that?" *Reemie whispers.*

"That's my boy's wife."

"Hook me up."

"Chill, I told you she fucks with my man."

"Your man not mines," *Reemie replies.*

Aisha has finished ringing up the items. She looked out for Tony. She only charged him $500 for everything. He has two pair of Timberlands and a Gerry ski coat, which alone comes to $500. He also has 5 pairs of jeans and 5 sweatshirts.

"That's a little something to get you started."

"Good looking out," *says Reemie.*

"Alright later, Eesh."

While they're riding up the hill Reemie notices everything is different from the way he remembers it. Some of Newark's landmarks are no longer here, just big empty lots. All the black owned stores are gone. Puerto Rican stores have replaced them.

When they get to his block he realizes the only thing that hasn't changed is the raggedy house he grew up in. It's still the worst house on the block.

When they pull to the house Reemie takes notice of a skinny, black woman on the porch with an Aunt Jemima scarf on her head. They get closer but he still doesn't recognize her. When she spots Tony's car she jumps off the stairs and runs over to them, screaming, **"My baby home! My baby home!"**

Reemie gets out of the car. She runs up to him and tries to hug him. He pushes her away and steps back. He has to look her up and down once more before he realizes this is his mother. This isn't how he left her. She didn't look like this. What happened to her? Is she sick? These are just some of the questions he asked himself.

He finally hugs her. The tears are running down his face. He's not crying because he's happy to see her, he's crying because he now realizes that the drugs have taken over her life.

CHAPTER 33

It's New Years Eve. In another hour it will be 1990.

It's a Saturday night. The Peppermint Lounge is packed. Besides it being New Years Eve, Reemie's boys Cool Breeze and O Drama have given Reemie a surprise coming home party.

Reemie's friends have come from all over. Besides his local friends from Newark, East Orange, Orange, and Irvington, he has boys that he was locked up with, who came all the way from Atlantic City, Camden, and Asbury. The females you wouldn't believe, they look like video models. Every hustler in the bar is wearing mink coats and alligator shoes. They're pulling up in all kinds of cars; some have even pulled up in limousines. It definitely a player's affair. It's so crowded. You can feel the tension in the air. Most of the tension is coming from the Jersey City (Chill Town) crowd. They are at least thirty deep.

Chill Town cats don't really get along with Newark niggas. The grudge came from years ago, when stick up kids from Newark would go over to Jersey City and stick them up. Whenever they're in the presence of Newark niggas they always act like they have something to prove.

E didn't really want to come because him and Cool Breeze can't stand each other, so he doesn't want to be around him. The only reason they came is because Tony begged them to.

Reemie is in a circle of nothing but women. Every nigga he knows is bringing a different girl over to meet him. He loves it. After all he went to jail when he was a kid. He was too busy getting into trouble. He didn't have time for girls, so now he's making up for what he missed.

Cool Breeze and O-Drama are sitting in the corner

observing everybody. They're the center of attention. Everybody is breaking their necks to get over there to them.

While Tony, Du and E hang around the bar, Reemie calls Tony over to him, **"Lil Cuzzo, come here for a minute!"** *Tony walks over to Reemie. Cool Breeze and O-Drama are standing with him.*

"Cuzzo this O-Drama and Cool Breeze. Ya'll this Cuzzo. Everybody calls him Nephew."

"What up, Cuzzo?" O-Drama asks. **"You don't mind if I call you that do you?"** he asks, *as he shakes Tony's hand.*

"No, not at all."

Cool Breeze extends his hand to shake Tony's hand. **"What up, Nephew? Pleased to meet you."**

"Likewise," Tony replies.

"We have heard so much about you," says O-Drama.

"All good, I hope," Tony replies.

"Ahhh, some good, some bad, you know 60/40, you up," Cool Breeze says sarcastically. *He's speaking so sarcastic because for one, a lot of his customers are coming all the way down the hill to get coke from Tony's block and two, he knows Tony and E are best friends. He hates the fact that E is with his little sister.*

There's something about that O-Drama, but Tony can't quite figure it out. All he knows is, he feels uncomfortable around him.

Cool Breeze is a money getter; O-Drama does all his dirty work. He's like his hit man. If somebody is late paying Breeze what they owe him, or disrespects him, O cracks him. Tony wants Reemie to stay away from O, because O-Drama sniffs dope. You can see it in his face. He's a dope fiend with expensive clothes on.

Tony gives them the 'Peace' and walks back over to the bar. E and Du are at the bar sipping Ginger Ales. They never drink in public. They know drinking makes you lose focus, and being around these guys you have to be focused. You never know what's going to happen next.

One of the cats from Jersey City is on the dance floor going crazy. You can tell he has just come home from jail. He's as big

129

as a house. He's about the same size as Reemie, if he isn't a little bigger. He has stripped down to his tank top, showing off his size. He's dancing so wild that he bumps into whoever is in his way. No one is saying anything because they don't want problems with him. He's even pouring drinks on people. He's drunk out of his mind. Instead of calming him down, his friends continuously cheer him on, by screaming, **"Chill Town, represent, represent!"**

"So where are you from?" Tony asks.

"Linden," Natasha replies.

"Where do you work?"

"I work on Wall Street."

"Wall street, I never met anyone who worked on Wall St," Tony admits.

"How about you?"

"Huh?" Tony questions. *Tony didn't expect this question. He can't tell her he's a drug dealer.* **"Keys, I, I deal with keys," he stutters. "I'm a locksmith. What brings you here?" Tony asks.** *He's trying to change the subject. He doesn't want her to find out what kind of keys he really deals with.*

"I've heard so much about the Peppermint, so my friend and I decided to see what all the hype was about," she explains.

"Hold up; excuse me for a second please," says Tony. *Tony walks over to the bar, and orders a bottle of Don P. He slowly walks back over to the booth where the young lady is standing. She's impressed with Tony. A $300 bottle of champagne for a female he barely knows. She is well worth it. She's not your average, around the way girl.*

As he pours the champagne, and hands her the glass, the drunken kid from Jersey City bumps into her, causing her to spill her drink all over her dress. Instead of apologizing he pulls her close to him, hugs her, and squeezes her butt. She pushes him off and slaps his face. He's enraged. He tries to slap her but Tony steps in between them.

"Get the fuck out the way!" he slurs. "I'm about to fuck this bitch up."

"Your mother is a bitch," she replies defensively.

He tries to push Tony to the side but Tony isn't budging.
CRACK! *He sucker punches Tony. Tony didn't see the right hand coming. He stumbles to the wall, and the drunken kid swings two more times. One catches Tony in the jaw, causing his legs to get weak. Tony grabs the boy and pulls him close to him. He's dizzy from the punch. He's trying to wrestle with the boy but the boy is too strong and Tony's legs are wobbly.*

Du and E run to the back to rescue Tony. Du pulls the two boys apart. The drunken kid swings a wild haymaker at Du. Du ducks it, causing him to miss. He swings once again. Du ducks again and swings; he lands. The boy's knees buckle. As he stumbles backwards Du comes closer to him. By this time the Jersey City crew has them surrounded. One of them has positioned himself right behind Du. He's preparing to sneak Du, until O-Drama draws his gun. **Click click!** *He slides a bullet into the chamber.*

The music goes off. The crowd opens up. Everyone backs away except for the Jersey City entourage. Everyone freezes. Du and O-Drama lock eyes.

"Do you, baby boy!" **O-drama shouts,** *giving him the ok to finish the job.* **"Don't nobody touch him!"** **shouts O-Drama,** *as he waves the big chrome gun around.*

The boys from Jersey City aren't saying anything. They have their eyes on O. The drunken kid swings another haymaker catching Du on the bridge of his nose. Du stumbles and the kid rushes him trying to grab him. Du steps to the side and swings five times, right jab, left cross, right hook, left uppercut, followed by another left cross. The combination is beautiful. He hit him with all five punches, causing the boy to fall face first. He's knocked out cold. E and Tony begin kicking him and stomping him, while he lays there on the floor.

"That's right, teach him some manners!" **O-Drama shouts.** *The Jersey City niggas haven't made a move, but they're furious. It's not that they're punks. Some of them are born killers,*

131

but they know they're out numbered, and it's impossible for them to win. It would be the other way around if they were at home, in Chill Town.

"That's enough!" Cool Breeze shouts.

"Listen, this is our house. Don't come here disrespecting our house," says O. "Ya'll can go back over and finish dancing or chilling whatever it is that you were doing, but we're not having that bullshit. Either ya'll stay here in peace or you leave in pieces." *He raises his gun in the air and gestures the DJ to turn the music back on. As he puts his gun back on his waist, he gives Du a high five and then he walks back to his table as if nothing has happened.*

The Chill Town crew hangs around for another twenty minutes, just long enough to let their boy recuperate from the knock out, before they exit the bar.

Tony admires how O-Drama handled the situation. The way he carries himself is so different. He doesn't have to speak much. His actions speak louder than his words. He's prepared to pull that trigger at any given moment and he doesn't have to get excited to do it.

The rest of the night everyone continued to party without a problem. After the bar closed, everyone met up at the East Orange Diner. O-Drama told every one to keep their guns on them just in case the chill town niggas came back to retaliate. They never showed up though.

After eating everyone went their separate ways. E went home to Aisha, while Tony and Du left with the two girls from Linden.

CHAPTER 34

Reemie has only been home for two months and things have changed drastically. Tony put him charge of everything. He's the enforcer. He's there to keep everybody in line, and make sure they do what they're supposed to.

Reemie cleared the whole block up. His saying is "if you're not with us, you are against us." He held a big meeting, telling everyone if they weren't taking work from Cuzzo, they can't work out there. Everybody is aware of the gun collection Tony's team has, plus nobody really knows what limits Reemie will take it to, so they're afraid to go up against him.

Even Auntie has straightened up. She's in the rehab. Reemie made her clean her act up.

No one works out of the apartment anymore. That's the first thing he changed. He has lookouts on both corners. The team is banging out of the abandoned building next door. They boarded all the entrances except for one secret entrance they only know about. They even have a crack head on the roof with a nine-millimeter, just in case stick up comes through. They sell the dime jugs out of the basement side window. (A jug is a small brown medicine bottle.)

Tony has the jugs packed with cocaine. Everybody comes for the jugs; even drug dealers. They can break them down and make 2 1/2 regular dimes out of one of his dimes. They don't even have to go to New York. They can almost triple their money, buying jugs on Tony's block. Tony has the block off the hook. He runs through three pies (kilo's) a week.

CHAPTER 35

2:30 a.m.

Tony parks in the alleyway of Flaco's house, and jumps out of the caravan. Usually, Tony doesn't work this late. He will be busy all tomorrow, so he has to handle this A.S.A.P.

Flaco takes a little longer than usual to answer the bell. He must be sleep, Tony thinks to himself. He rings it again, this time he leans on the bell. Tony looks up and he sees Flaco peeking out the window.

"Here I come," he yells. *As Flaco is coming down the stairs, Tony continuously peeks around to make sure no one is watching him.*

Flaco opens the door and Tony rushes in. Flaco leads Tony up the stairs, half sleep. They're both tiptoeing up the stairs. They don't want to wake up the other tenants.

Once they enter the living room, Tony notices Flaco already has two and a half kilos piled up on the coffee table.

Now Tony flips once a week. Flaco told him it's better to buy what you need for the week instead of running back and fourth. This way he eliminates his risk of getting locked up.

Tony is doing splendid, ever since Reemie came home. He was already doing his thing, but now that he has someone to watch his back, he feels comfortable enough to step his game all the way up.

"Flaco, I'm not going to check every one of these. It's too late, I can't waste any time."

"Yeah, I don't usually work this late either, but I did it for you."

"Are they white?" Tony asks. "You know I can't fuck with that beige shit."

"Yeah, snow white."

Tony pulls the backpack off his back, and unzips it. He pulls the shopping bag out. In the shopping bag there is $57,500.

He packs the work in his backpack, zips it up and grabs it by the straps.

"Here's the money," **he says,** *as he hands Flaco the bag.* **"I'll call you next week,"** **he says,** *as he walks out the door.*

"Alright," Flaco replies, *still half sleep.*

Flaco locks the door behind Tony.

Before Tony opens the outside door, he pulls the 9mm off his waist and puts it in his right coat pocket. Holding his finger on the trigger, he cracks the door slowly. He peeks to the right then to the left. After seeing that the coast is clear, he walks quickly to the van and pulls off.

There isn't much traffic on the streets, being that it's so late. Tony is driving extra careful.

As he's riding up Tremont Avenue, he spots a police car coming towards him. They pass each other but Tony can see the cop car's brake lights through the rear view mirror. The cop hasn't stopped yet. He's just riding extra slow. Tony, steps on the gas a little bit, still keeping his eyes on the rear view mirror.

He's busting a U-turn. Tony gets nervous, and speeds up even more. The cop is gaining on him. Tony turns his blinker on and makes a left turn onto Munn, just to see if he is following him. The officer turns right behind him. Tony starts fumbling with the book bag. He unzips the bag. The loud aroma fills the car instantly. He finally gets the shopping bag out and lays it on his lap. The cop car is close on Tony's bumper. He's probably running the license plates. Tony sticks his hand under the cushion of the seat and fumbles around for the switch. The cop turns his lights on. He's pulling Tony over. **"Oh shit!"** **Tony blurts out.** *Tony continues to ride as if he didn't hear the officer. He flicks the switch.*

"Whoop, whoop! *He hits the sirens. Tony slows down. He watches the door, as the metal box slides out from it. Tony dumps the bag inside the box and flicks the switch.*

"**Pull over,**" **the cop says,** *over the loud speaker. Tony pulls in front of Bradley Court and pulls over. Oh shit! My gun, Tony thinks. He reaches in his pocket and flicks the switch with his other hand. The officer is already out the car, walking towards Tony's van. The box opens up; Tony dumps the gun and flicks the switch. The officer is already at the window as the box is closing.*

"**You didn't see me trying to pull you over?**"

"**No, I didn't sir.**"

"**We the only two cars out here, I got these bright lights flashing and my sirens on, and you didn't notice anything?**"

"**No sir, my head was somewhere else.**"

"**Yeah ok, license, registration and insurance.**"

Tony reaches in the glove compartment, and snatches the papers out. As he hands the papers over, the cop asks, "**Where are you coming from this late?**"

Tony hesitates before answering. "**From work.**"

"**Where do you work?**"

"**Shoprite, I work from 6 pm to 2 am.**"

"**This tint on your window is mighty dark. Wait right here,**" **he instructs,** *as he walks back to his car.*

The officer has been sitting in his car for about five minutes so far. Tony isn't worried. All of his paper work is good. Tony is sitting there bopping his head to imaginary music. He's trying to act as confident as he can.

The officer finally gets out and approaches the car. Tony sticks his hand out of the window, thinking the officer is going to hand him the paper work, but instead the officer grabs the door handle and says, "**Please step out, sir.**"

"**Huh?**"

"**Step out please.**" *Now Tony is worried. Tony steps out and the officer places his hands on Tony's shoulders and leads him to the police car. The officer opens the door, and gently pushes Tony in. Tony sits attentively in the police car, watching every move the police officer makes as he searches the van. He's looking in the trunk, under the seat; he has even lifted the hood. He's on his way* *back towards Tony but he quickly turns around and starts walking back to the van. This time he gets in and closes the door. After starting the van up, he steps on the accelerator. He listens as the engine races.*

The officer walks back to the police car, and opens the door for Tony to get out. He hands Tony the keys, and he steps closer and closer, until they're standing face to face. Tony can feel the air coming from the officer's nose as he exhales. **"You're free to go, Nephew."**

Tony thinks his ears are deceiving him. **"Nephew, you're clean right now, but I'm going to get you. You hear me?"**

"Nephew, who is Nephew?" *Tony asks.*

"You don't know who Nephew is? Mighty funny everybody else does." *He laughs as he walks back to the police car.*

For the rest of the ride Tony wonders how the police officer knew him. Someone is running off at the mouth.

CHAPTER 36

After a bunch of phone calls Reemie finally got in touch with his boy Buck-Wild. Buck-Wild was so happy to hear he was home. Reemie rushed to pick him up.

Buck-Wild told Reemie to meet him at the Dairy Queen, in North Newark on Bloomfield Avenue.

Reemie pulls up slowly. Buck is standing along side the curb. The windows on Reemie's car are so dark, that Reemie has to roll the passenger window down so Buck can recognize him. Buck jumps in quickly.

"What up, baby boy?" Buck-Wild asks.

Reemie looks him over before he replies. Buck looks terrible. The year he has on the street has really beat him down. When he left Trenton State Prison, he was built like a super hero, straight out of a comic book. All the ripping and running is really starting to take toll on him.

"What's the deal?" Reemie asks.

"You finally made it home, huh?" says Buck-Wild.

"Hell yeah!" Reemie replies. "I thought they were never letting me out of there." *Buck laughs.* "Them crackers broke me. They got ten years, that's it. They ain't getting no more from me. I ain't never going back."

"Word up," Buck agrees.

Reemie is driving with no destination.

"How have you been doing since the last time we spoke?" Reemie asks.

"Everything is alright, but my money is getting low. I'm going to have to make another move soon."

"Don't worry, I got you. I'm doing alright," Reemie

reassures.

"I hear that!"

They've been riding around for almost an hour, reminiscing about the time they did together in prison. Even though they were in prison they had so many fun times together.

These two guys are closer than brothers. They know everything about each other, even their deepest darkest secrets. Buck was the only person Reemie rolled with in Trenton. Reason being; Reemie knew Buck had his back regardless of what. One particular time Reemie was getting jumped by twelve guys from Camden; Buck came to his aid. Overall, they got beat down, but Buck shanked two of the guys up real bad. One of them almost didn't make it. He was on a life support machine and everything. Everyone thought Reemie had done it. They sent him to AD-SEG (lock up), but Buck stepped up and took the weight. Situations like that made them develop love for each other.

As they ride past People's Choice, Reemie suggests going in for a few drinks. Buck agrees.

Reemie parks. As they're getting out, Reemie asks, **"You're not dirty are you?"** *(Meaning does he have a gun on him.) Reemie is sure that was a stupid question, because Buck doesn't go anywhere without his gun. He has done so much dirt he doesn't know when someone will catch up with him.*

"Yeah, I'm dirty. You know I keep my shit on me!" Buck shouts.

"We can't go in there with guns on us. Security will frisk us at the door. We'll just leave the guns in the car. I'll back up, so we'll be closer to the bar, just in case something kicks off."

They walk to the trunk, peek around, pull their guns off their waist and stash them in the trunk.

At the door the officer frisks them, just like Reemie said they would. They walk to the back and sit down. The bar is empty. There are only eight other people in there besides them.

"What are you drinking?" Reemie asks.

"E&J."

"Bartender, two E&J's with coke."

The bartender comes right back with the drinks. They begin sipping and talking. Before Reemie realized it, they had drunk four rounds.

He's feeling nice. He's not too drunk. He's feeling a little groovy, but Buck is fucked up. He's not a heavy drinker. Reemie can tell he's drunk by the way his words are beginning to slur.

"Bartender, one more round!" Reemie shouts. *As soon as the drink gets there, Buck guzzles it straight down. Reemie doesn't get a chance to touch his.* "Here take this one too," Reemie offers. "I'll order another one." *Buck guzzles this one down even quicker than the last one. Instead of ordering another drink, Reemie just sits there listening to Buck babble.*

"Reemie, you my nigga. You know that?" he asks, *as he puts his arm around Reemie's neck.*

"Yeah, I know."

"You better know," he slurs. "I love you. I'll die for you."

"Same here," Reemie confirms.

"I will kill for you," says Buck. *He spit in Reemie's face as he spoke.* "Do you want me to kill somebody for you? Point them out. Where they at? Do you want me to kill somebody in this bar?"

"Nah Buck, chill!" *Reemie is convinced that Buck is fully drunk now.*

"I'm tired of my life!" Buck shouts. "Sometimes I wake up, and I say to myself, I want to change, but as soon as I get outside, it's the same shit all over again. I'm tired of hurting motherfuckers."

"Well stop hurting motherfuckers!"

"How will I eat? Do you expect me to stand on the corner? I'm not with that clocking shit," he slurs. "I want to change but it ain't easy. When I go to a motherfucker and ask him for help, he gives me the run around. I ain't got it right now, or give me two weeks, but when I come to a nigga with that gun in my hand, I get more than I really need. **Punks only respect pressure. Always remember that. Do you hear me?**"

"**Yeah I hear you.**"

"**Reemie, I would never cross you. I don't give a fuck if you had a trillion dollars, and I was starving. I would never hurt you. I love you.**" *He hugs Reemie tight and kisses him on the cheek.*

"**I love you, too.**"

"**Last call for alcohol!**" **shouts the DJ.**

Reemie and Buck step away from the bar. Reemie has to help Buck out the door.

When Reemie gets Buck inside the car, he takes notice that Buck's pants are wet. He has pissed on himself.

Reemie gets in the car and drives off.

Five minutes into the ride, Reemie looks over at Buck; he's knocked out. It's 3:00 AM, not a soul is on the street. There's no traffic. The buses have stopped running over an hour ago.

Reemie makes the right turn onto the Bully. (Dr. Martin L. King Blvd) Buck-Wild is still asleep. He pulls in front of the apartment building and two men walk up to the car. As they open the door, Buck wakes up. He sits up quickly, and glances at the two men. He then looks straight ahead. He rubs his eyes to get his vision together.

"**Who are they?**" **Buck whispers.**

"**These my peoples!**" **says Reemie.**

They're cruising up the block. Buck is sitting up. He's on point. He's sure Reemie will never cross him, but he doesn't trust the other two guys. Still feeling groovy, he looks at Reemie out of one eye, and asks, "**Where are we going?**"

"**For a ride.**" *Buck doesn't like the sound of that.*

"**A ride where?**"

"**Buck, I want you to meet someone. This right here,**" he says, *while pointing to the man behind the driver's seat.* "**Is my little cousin Tony, but you can call him nephew. I think ya'll already met, but I want to formally introduce ya'll.**"

Buck looks back. When he sees Tony's face, he realizes what's going on. His buzz has worn off. Buck begins to fumble for his gun. Reemie is looking straight ahead but he's watching attentively out the corner of his eye.

"Your gun is in the trunk; remember?" *Buck forgot, but now it's starting to come back to him. At this moment Buck realizes this is going to be his last ride. He knows he has to say something quick, to make them change their minds.*

"I swear to God I didn't know! I would never cross your family. We're brothers. What hurts you hurts me," *he pleads.*

Reemie continues to drive as if Buck hasn't said a word. He's looking straight ahead.

"Nephew, Tony, listen. I didn't know we were family."

Tony listens, without saying a word. He's not that tough after all. He's a punk, Tony thinks to himself. In the apartment he was so aggressive. The sight of him makes Tony furious. All the pain he put him through; the beating, the violating and the sleepless nights. Tony is ready to do him right now.

"Reemie, we got too much time in, let's straighten this out."

The man in the other seat is O-Drama. He hasn't said a word. He's just listening. Tony didn't want him there but he just happened to be with Reemie, when Reemie got in contact with Buck.

"Straighten it out, how?" *Reemie asks.*

"I will give him the money back."

"It's not about the money, it's the principle," *Reemie* **explains.**

The more Buck begs the angrier Tony becomes. He's looking for mercy but in the apartment he showed no mercy at all.

"Please man, I. ...... *SMACK! Before he gets the rest of the sentence out, Tony smacks him across the head with his .45.* **"Aghhh! Please!"** *he begs.*

"Shut the fuck up and stop begging!" *SMACK! He smacks him again. The blood drips from his head. His collar is soaked with blood. Reemie pulls up to the entrance of Vailsburg*

Park. He stops and turns the lights off.

"Reemie, is this how you gonna do it? All the time we got together. You gonna kill me? I just told you I would never hurt you, no matter what," **Buck says,** *with tears in his eyes.* "We fought too many wars together. We cried too many tears together. Think about the nights we had no food; we had to split one can of soup."

Reemie isn't looking at him. He's staring straight ahead. The hot tears burn as they roll down his face.

"Please don't kill me," **Buck begs.**

Reemie opens the door. "I love you!" **he shouts,** *as he gets out. He can't stand the sight of seeing his man go out like this.*

"Reemie, please!" *It's about to go down. Buck is sure they're about to kill him. He's scared. He doesn't know what to do. He tries to make a get away. As he attempts to open the door,* **BOOM! BOOM!** *Buck's head crashes into the dashboard. Tony can't believe it, O –Drama has just killed Buck-Wild.*

O- Drama finally speaks. "Hurry up; get him out of the car!" *Tony climbs from the backseat and runs to the passenger's seat.*

As Tony grabs the door, O screams, "Don't touch him, your fingerprints."

Reemie opens the driver's door. He leans inside, puts his foot on Buck's shoulder and kicks him out of the car. Reemie jumps in the driver's seat, while Tony gets in the backseat.

Reemie speeds off recklessly. Tony looks up front. The whole side is covered with blood. O-Drama sits there cool and calm. Tony has so many thoughts running through his head. He replays Buck's head banging into the dashboard, over and over again.

They're riding alongside the Parkway. As they approach the entrance, O- Drama calmly says, "Turn your lights on."

Tony looks behind him. There are no cops; a clean get away.

On the Parkway, Reemie is driving the normal speed

143

limit. O still hasn't said a word. He's sitting there acting as if nothing happened, just bopping his head to the music. Tony is now convinced that this man is a born killer.

Reemie is hurting inside. He just set up the only person who showed him love over the past years. He had to go. He crossed the family.

Reemie gets off at the Lyons Avenue exit. He's dropping O-Drama off first. He's not pulling up to a house. O told Reemie to let him out at the gas station on Springfield Avenue. He doesn't want Tony to know where he lives, but little does he know Reemie told Tony weeks ago that O is staying in the Marshall Apartments with some girl. That's only one of the places where he stays. Before O gets out, Tony screams, **"Thanks O!"**

"Don't worry about it, baby boy! Real niggas do real things."

"Anything you need, don't hesitate to ask," Tony offers.

"Alright," O replies, *while slowly nodding his head up and* down. **"Later ya'll!"** *he shouts, as he gets out of the car.*

Reemie pulls off. He hasn't said a word since the shooting.

"Reemie, are you alright?"

"Na Cuzzo, I feel like shit. Seeing my man begging me to spare his life, that shit hurts. He was the only nigga that had my back in prison; and when he got home he took care of me just like he said he would. The only reason I let this happen was it was you he violated. If it were anybody else, I would have never done it. You see I had to get out of the car, I couldn't watch that shit. Now I have to go to a funeral and stand over my man, knowing I'm responsible for him being there. How will I face his mother and his sister? They love me. Down the joint, they used to bring me bigger food packages, than they brought him. Every month his mother baked me a German Chocolate cake, and every birthday they sent me a gift. Even after he went home, they were still bringing me food packages, and visiting me. My own mother didn't even visit me!" *The tears roll down his face.*

"I know that was your man and all, but I was going to kill him with or without ya'll. He violated me. Do you know how it feels to be taped up and gagged, not knowing when these motherfuckers are going to kill you? They running around your house looking through all your personal shit, and you can't do nothing. Punk ass niggas pistol-whipping you, taking advantage of you because at that moment they got the upper hand." *The more Tony talks, the angrier he becomes.* "Fuck that bitch ass nigga! He crossed me. I ain't got no sympathy for that nigga. You heard what he said; if he knew we were family he would have never done that. So basically what he was saying was fuck me. So I'm saying fuck him! Reemie, I'm not going to let myself be put in a position like that ever again. From here on out, if I feel threatened by a nigga, if I even get the word that a nigga got plans of hurting me and mines, I'll kill him and his whole family. If they hurt one of mine, I gotta hurt two of theirs! When I first started this hustling shit, I didn't know it was this serious. All I wanted to do was make me a little money for school. You know, I had one foot in, and one foot out. Jokers peeped me. They thought I was just a little schoolboy. They tried to take advantage of me. They robbed me, they shot me, and they even tried to extort me, but guess what, I ain't going nowhere. Through all the money, the madness, the murder, I'm still here. The streets created this monster. Now I got my game face on, and I got both feet in. These cats ain't got no love for me, and I ain't got no love for them. And anybody who gets in the way of me seeing the big picture, I'm gonna murder his ass. I'm getting rid of all problems. So like I said, fuck your man! You're sitting here feeling sorry for this motherfucker like he was a good guy. The nigga caused me pain. How about he would have killed me in there, then what? Man, fuck him! You said it yourself, if a nigga ain't with us, he's against us."

"Cuzzo, you don't understand."

"Understand what?" Tony asks. "No, you don't

understand!"

For the remainder of the ride neither of them said a word. They just gazed out of the window.

They went to Reemie's apartment and took it down for a few hours.

CHAPTER 37

Later that afternoon

E and Du have just stepped into the apartment. They're attempting to wake Tony. Reemie is already out back cleaning the car up.

"Tony! Tony! Wake up!" **Du shouts.** *Tony opens one eye, and looks around*

"What's up?" **he asks,** *with a groggy voice.*

"Damn baby, you don't ever sleep this late. You're the one always telling me the early bird gets the worm; now look at you," says E.

"I had a long ass night," Tony replies. "Where ya'll headed?"

"To the barbershop," E replies.

"Hold up, I'm going I need a buzz, too."

Tony hurries to the bathroom to get himself together, as they wait for him in the jeep.

Before leaving Tony goes out back to give Reemie the keys to his van. He doesn't want Reemie driving around in that car after what happened. Tony had already decided not to tell his boys what happened. He feels like he's betraying them but he also knows everything isn't for everybody.

As soon as they walk into Bomber's Barber Shop on 12th Ave and 8th St, all they hear in the air is Buck-Wild this and Buck-Wild that. It hasn't been twelve hours and the whole town already knows. Everything the people are saying is a bunch of lies. They're telling all kinds of rumors of who killed Buck. That's one thing Tony is glad about, judging by the stories they're telling, he's sure they don't have a clue as to who killed Buck. E's response was, 'luckily they got to him before we did.' That let Tony know that E is as much in the dark as everyone else. You can see happiness on everyone's face. They no longer have to worry about Buck-Wild.

While the barber is finishing Du's hair, E and Tony wait outside.

"**We got the money ready. It's in the trunk,**" says E.

"**Are you getting the whole pie?**" *(Kilo)*

"**Yeah!**" E replies.

"**Damn, ya'll doing alright.**"

"**Yeah, ever since I stopped cutting the coke, shit picked up.**"

"**I told you it would,**" says Tony. "**I won't be able to make the move till later. Reemie has my van and I'm not moving birds around without a stash spot, especially after that cop called me Nephew.**"

"**Just take the money and call me when you get it,**" E suggests.

As Du walks out the shop, a black 850 BMW pulls up right in front of E's jeep. Cool Breeze and O-Drama get out.

Everyone gets quiet as they step onto the curb. O-Drama gets there first. He shakes all of their hands, but he hugs Tony. "**What's up, Nephew?**"

"**What's up, O?**" *They're both acting as if they hadn't seen each other in a while.*

Breeze walks up. He half shakes Tony's hand and walks right past E. As he passes they stare in each other's eyes. Cool Breeze doesn't like E, because he doesn't want him and Aisha together. He told Aisha, E is a fake ass nigga. Every time Cool Breeze sees E he gives him long cold stares.

E and Du walk to the jeep, while Tony stands there conversing with O. "**What's up, O?**"

"**You know, I was thinking about what you said about if I ever need something. Well, I know what you could do for me.**"

"**Anything O, just name it.**"

"**Well, Reemie told me you got that flavor shit on the yay-yo tip (cocaine). Why don't you bring us in on the**

148

connect?" *Tony hesitates to reply. He's almost sure this isn't O's idea. Breeze must have talked him into it.*

"Well my connect, he real funny about meeting people, but I'll see what I can do."

"Oh, he's one of them kind," says O. "One of them scary ass niggas, huh? What number are you getting them at?"

Tony isn't about to tell them his personal business. "That depends on what you're buying. What number are ya'll getting them for?"

"Breeze, come here!" *Breeze walks over.*

"What up, baby?"

"What's the number on that bird?" O asks.

"Right now I'm paying $24,000 a joint but the shit is so-so. It ain't like the shit they got down the hill."

"Check it out," says Tony. "I'm going to get up with my peoples and see if I can pull some strings."

"Yeah do that, because I'm good for at least three joints a week."

"I know the price isn't going to be much different though," says Tony.

"No problem, as long as it's the right shit."

All Tony sees is $$$$$ dollar signs. He can sell them to Breeze for $24,000 and make a $3,000 profit off each pie, because he only pays $21,000 for a pie. If Breeze buys three a week that will be $9,000 profit every time they do business. "How soon would you be ready?" Tony asks greedily.

"I'm ready when you are. I was about to make a move, but if you can guarantee that he'll do it, I'll wait."

"Let me talk to him. I'll call you in about two hours and let you know what's up," says Tony.

"That's a bet," Breeze replies.

"Alright later ya'll!" Tony shouts.

"Later baby boy," says O. "Thanks a lot."

"Don't thank me. Real niggas do real things, that's what you told me right?"

"That's right, one hand washes the other," says O. *They both laugh.*

Tony made them feel like he's doing them a favor, when in reality he's only looking out for himself.

O and Breeze walk into Bombers, and Tony jumps in the jeep.

Before Tony could get inside, they begin firing questions at him.

"What the fuck them sneaky ass niggas talking about?" E asks.

"Nothing really."

"I don't like them motherfuckers. They're sneaky as hell," Du admits.

"Yeah you can see it all over their faces," E agrees. Aisha told me Breeze is always asking questions about me. I told her not to tell him shit about me.

Tony is sitting quietly, just listening. He was going to tell them about the conversation, but after hearing how much they despise those guys, he decides to keep it to himself. Tony doesn't like the fact that he's been keeping so many secrets from them but it seems like the further he gets in the game, the more secretive he gets.

CHAPTER 38

When Tony arrives, back to the apartment, Reemie is parked out front. He's sitting on the passenger side with the windows rolled down, listening to the radio.

Tony jumps in the driver's seat and tosses the money E gave him into the back seat. They're off to see Flaco. Tony usually doesn't take anyone with him when he goes to see Flaco, but he isn't thinking. The only thing he has on his mind is the $9,000 profit he's going to make off Breeze.

"Your peoples want to do business with me," says Tony. "What do you think?"

"My peoples who?"

"O-Drama and Breeze, do you think they alright?"

"Yeah, they cool but I'll be right there with you when you do business with them, anyway."

"Nah, I just wanted to get the ok from you. Do me a favor?" Tony asks, *as he hands him his cellular phone.* "Dial this number for me."

"What is it?" Reemie asks.

"917-563-0824," Tony says slowly. "Did it beep yet?"

"Yeah."

"Put my number in and hit the star button and then press 1000."

Reemie does exactly what Tony instructed him to do before hanging up the phone. That's the code Tony uses to let Flaco know he's on his way and to have one kilo ready. That's what the 1000 stands for, 1000 grams. (Actually each kilo weighs 1008 grams)

As they turn down South Street, Flaco's house is the third house on the block.

Tony pulls in the alleyway of the apartment, while Reemie just leans back in the seat glancing around. Tony grabs the bag of money and dashes out of the van.

"Squat right there, I'll be back in twenty minutes."

"Alright, Cuzzo."

Tony rings the bell and Flaco lets him right in.

"Who is that in the van with you?" Flaco asks.

"That's only my cousin; he's cool."

"You know that's bad business poppy."

"Nah, he's alright. If he wasn't I wouldn't bring him around here."

"Ok, I'm going to take your word for it."

"Do you have it ready?" Tony asks.

"Yeah, it's ready.

Tony hands him the bag of money.

"$21,000, right?" Flaco asks.

"Yep, oh another thing I need to talk to you about. I got a kid who wants to do some things. He gets a lot of money up there in the Vailsburg section. He got that part of town on lock. Niggas can't do nothing without him saying so. And the ones who ain't working for him have to buy weight from him or they can't sell it around his area."

"Oh yeah," Flaco interrupts.

"Yeah, I told him I was going to see what I could do about putting ya'll together."

"No Poppy, I don't need that heat."

"Nah, I'm not going to let him see you or nothing. I just want you to back me up."

"Back you up how?" Flaco questions.

"Well, he buys a lot of kilos. If I can't fill the order, I'll need you to back me."

"Yeah?"

"If it's possible you could give them to me when he calls, then I'll go meet him and bring your money right back to you."

Tony waits for Flaco's response. Tony doesn't think Flaco will trust him with three birds, but to his surprise, Flaco tells him he will do it. "Are you sure?" Tony asks.

"Why wouldn't I be? Tony, I trust you. When will the guy be ready?"

"He's ready right now. Wait, let me call him to make sure."

Tony pulls out his phone and dials O-drama's phone number.

"Hello," O shouts.

"O, this is Tony, are you with Breeze?"

"Yeah, he right here; hold on." *Breeze gets on the phone.*

"Breeze, I'm with my peoples now. What's up?"

"I told you, I'm ready when you are."

"You said you want three, right?"

"Yeah, what's the price on them?"

"I told you they would be $24,000."

"Alright, call me when you ready," says Breeze.

"I'll hit you later." *Tony hangs up the phone.* "He said he's ready whenever we are."

"Well, I got three right here." *Flaco opens the safe. It has to be at least 12 kilos piled up in there. Tony has never seen this many birds at one time.*

"Here, take them with you."

Tony packs the four birds in his shopping bag. "As soon as I meet with him, I'll call you." *Tony hurries out the door.*

As Tony walks out the door, he notices Reemie watching the bag. Reemie watches the bag from the doorway all the way to the truck.

When Tony gets in Reemie already has the stash spot opened for him. Tony drops the work in the box and pulls off.

CHAPTER 39

As they pull up to Breeze's house, they can see that the front of the building is crowded. He lives in the Elizabeth Towers on Elizabeth Ave.

While entering the building, Tony places his right hand inside his pocket where he has his 9-millimeter. Reemie is carrying the bag with the 4 pies in it. Before they could get to the lobby everyone starts yelling, Kareem! They all run over to him like he's a God. Reemie nonchalantly shakes their hands and keeps on stepping.

Once they step inside the elevator Tony asks who was all those people he spoke to. Reemie explained that he knew most of those guys from different prisons he had been in and how he took care of them and that is why they act like that when they see him. Reemie is well respected everywhere. There isn't one place they have been that people didn't treat him like royalty.

When they enter the apartment, Tony is shocked. He thought Breeze would be living better than this. You wouldn't imagine a nigga like him living in a rat hole like this. **"Have a seat," says Breeze,** while pointing to a welfare type living room set. The best thing in the whole apartment is the big screen television.

O-Drama was sleep. He woke up when Reemie smacked him across the head.

Reemie passes the bag to Tony. Tony opens it up as everyone crowds around. Tony pulls his gun out of his coat pocket and puts it on his waist. He purposely let them see it, just in case they had other plans. After he pulls the three kilos out, Breeze immediately starts examining them.

"Do you mind if I cook a piece up?" Breeze asks.

"**No, not at all, do whatever you have to,**" **Tony replies**.
Breeze breaks a tiny piece off the brick and weighs it.
"**Four grams,**" **he says.** *He passes it to O.*

O takes the rock to the stove. He puts the rock inside a small jar and adds baking soda. He then places the jar inside a boiling pot of water. Tony has his attention on Breeze as he examines the work.

O-Drama snatches the jar out of the boiling water and starts shaking the jar in the air. All you hear is, tick, tick, tick. That's the sound of the rock banging against the jar. "**Do you hear that?**" **O asks.** "**It got hard in no time.**"

O empties the jar onto a plate and Breeze checks it out.
"**She came back white as hell, too,**" **says Breeze.** *He then places the rock back on the scale. The scale reads 4.4.* "**It didn't lose shit either. Matter of fact, 4 extra lines came back.**" *That means the cocaine is as pure as a bunch of ghetto niggas can get it.* "**If it had cut on it, the cut would have dissolved in the water. Yeah, this is definitely the shit we need!**" **Breeze shouts.** "**O, hand him that bag.**" *O passes the bag to Tony.*

Tony and Reemie start counting. Tony notices O-Drama chopping up a little rock. After chopping it very fine, he dumps the powder onto a dollar bill and starts sniffing away. Nobody is even paying attention to him. This must be routine, Tony assumes.

Tony has his gun on his lap under the table as he counts the money. They have the money separated $10,000 per stack. 500, $20 dollars bills in each stack. In total they counted $70,000.

"**That's only $70,000!**" **Tony shouts.** *He looks at Breeze; he's trying not to stare at O, who has been sniffing the whole time.*

"**Are you sure?**"
"**I'm positive!**"
"**It should be in there!**" **Breeze shouts.** *Tony hands the money back to Breeze so he can check it for himself.*

"**Did you see the stack of 50's?**" **Breeze asks.**
"**No,**" **Tony replies.**

Tony senses a little funny business. He grabs his gun under the table. Reemie notices him with the gun in his hand. He taps him under the table and shakes his head no. Tony isn't trying to hear him. He thinks they're trying to play him.

"Yo, cut the shit! Where's the 2 grand?" Reemie asks.

"I'm not bullshitting, it's supposed to be in there," Breeze explains. *Tony then rises up with the gun in his hand. Breeze looks at him and says,* "O, did you see the stack of 50's?"

O stops sniffing for a second and looks at Tony with the chrome 9mm in his hand. "Oh, I got it right here," he says, *as he walks over to the table. His eyes are cherry red. The residue from the cocaine is all over his nose. He's still making the sniffing noise as he hands Tony the money.*

"My fault, Nephew."

"Don't worry about it," says Tony, *as he puts his gun back on his waist.*

Tony and Reemie walk to the door. "Later ya'll! Reemie shouts.

"Alright later," says Breeze. "Nephew, I'll be calling you in about 5 days."

O continues to sniff away. He hasn't looked up.

Getting off the elevator they pass a crowd of people in the lobby. Tony watches everyone. If anyone comes anywhere near them he's prepared to shoot.

Neither of them speak until they get in the car.

"Your man tried to play me out," says Tony.

"Nah, they were just trying to test you. You did right. Now they know you ready for whatever. I knew what they were doing that's why I told you not to do anything crazy. Them boys won't dare cross me. They know I don't play!"

It only takes them ten minutes to get to the apartment. As Tony pulls in front he hands Reemie the stack of 50's. "What's this Cuzzo?"

"Two grand."

"For what?"

"For nothing."

Reemie stuffs the money in his coat pocket and gets out of the car. Reemie has a loss of words. Tony gave him $2,000 for nothing. Reemie doesn't know where he would be if it weren't for Tony.

As Tony tries to pull off, the crack heads gather around his car. Nephew, can I get one for eight? Nephew this, and Nephew that. Tony just answers yes to everything and speeds off. He has to meet E and Du. They're waiting for their work.

CHAPTER 40

"What the fuck is taking Tony so long?" E asks, *as they sit in the jeep waiting for Tony.*

"For real," Du agrees.

"He acts like we don't have shit to do but wait out here for his slow ass. He's probably somewhere taking his sweet old time," says E. "If it ain't about Tony, it don't matter to him."

"Yeah, that's how he's been acting lately."

"Yeah, I peeped him too; he's been acting real funny," E replies.

"Yeah, everything is a big secret with him."

E spots Tony's van pulling up. Tony parks and gets out the van. As Tony gets in with them, E speaks, "Got damn Big Time! We've been waiting out here for a long time."

Tony hears the sarcasm in his voice; so he snaps.

"Ya'll ain't the only motherfuckers I gotta see! If you can't wait, get your shit from somewhere else!"

Du and E look at each other. They can't believe Tony is acting like this towards them.

"It ain't that serious!" Du shouts. "We just saying it don't look good sitting out here waiting all that time, that's all."

"I'm tired of all that complaining shit."

"Are you alright?" Du asks. "You have been acting funny as hell."

"Word up!" E agrees.

Tony leans his head back, with his eyes closed. "Yeah man, I'm alright. I'm just under a lot of pressure. I apologize for snapping on you E, but I've been going crazy lately. Ever since that house robbery I haven't been the same. It's hard for me to trust motherfuckers. All day long I'm watching my mirrors. If I'm in the store and someone walks too close to me I reach for my gun. I can't even get into a bitch, because I think she's trying to set me up. I can't even sleep at night. All night long I'm back and forth looking out the window. Shit crazy, ya'll don't understand."

"Maybe you need to slow down a little," Du suggests.

"Slow down? I can't do that! I never dreamed about making this much money in my life. I can't stop now; I'm in too deep." *Tony lays there quietly as Du checks over the work.* "Let me get out of here, I got a few things to do."

"Later baby, take it easy," Du shouts.

E doesn't respond. He's just sitting there wearing a serious mad face.

Once they pull off E finally speaks.

"Fuck that nigga! He think he big time now cause he's getting a little cash. He tried to shine on me! I used to take care of him back when he was Ronald McDonald. Now he's "Nephew" he forgot where the fuck he came from."

Du senses the jealousy in E's voice. All the things E dreamed of doing Tony is really doing them. E hates the fact that they have to go through Tony to get their work and they have been on the streets longer than him.

"Chill E, the man is stressed out. Look at all the shit he's been through, shootouts, robberies, murders, everything. You know he's really not that kind of guy. The streets forced him to be like that."

"Well if he can't stand the heat, he needs to get the hell out of the kitchen!" E shouts. "I know what I'm going to do; I'm going to make some calls. He ain't the only one who got connections. I'm not fucking with him no more, and if you want to fuck with him, then I ain't fucking with you either."

"So you're going to let our friendship end over money?"

"Yeah, over money!" E replies. "I mean, we still can be boys, but I can't fuck with him on the money tip."

Du doesn't like the sound of this. E has a lot of jealousy in his heart. Everything was ok when Tony was a broke ass schoolboy trailing behind E, but now that the tables have turned E can't handle it.

E and Du proceed to the smoke shop, to get empty bottles so they can bag up and drop the work off to JJ.

Tony drives right back to Flaco's house to give him the $63,000 he owes him. That was the fastest $9,000 profit he had ever made. He noticed a different look in Flaco's eyes. Even the way Flaco talked to him was different. He didn't talk down to him. For the first time he talked to him like an equal. Tony figured it out; the more money you make the more respect you get.

As Tony gets back in the van he talks on the phone with his mother. After he concludes the conversation he lays the phone on the passenger seat. He notices a small white wrapper on the seat. He dusts it off onto the floor, leaving a trail of powder on the seat. Tony pulls over, picks up the wrapper and examines it. To his surprise it's a bag of dope. Tony can't figure out who could have left it in his van. Then Reemie comes into his head. Nah, Reemie isn't the type to get high, but no one else had been in the van. Tony knows he has to get to the bottom of this.

CHAPTER 41

---

*Two months have passed. The summer has rolled back
around. Everybody is getting money. Everyone is happy except
E. He didn't have any luck finding a new connect, so he has to
continue getting work from Tony.*

*Cool Breeze is killing them on his side of town. He stepped
it up. He now buys four birds at a time.*

*As for Reemie, Tony never mentioned the bag of dope to
him. He decided to just observe him. He's on the look out for any
warning signs.*

*Reemie is getting money. Besides the money Tony pays him
for watching over the block, Reemie has his boys coming up from
Atlantic City and Asbury Park buying a half- a kilo at a time. Each
time they come Tony and Reemie split the profit.*

*Auntie is out of the rehab. She looks beautiful. She gained
her weight back, and she has false teeth in her mouth. She also got
her old job back. She's a courtroom stenographer, in the courts
down town.*

*Everything is going fine until one hot afternoon Du calls
Tony's phone talking loud and acting hysterical.*

"Hello?"

"Tone, Tone can you hear me?"

"Who is this?"

"It's Du! Can you hear me?"

"Stop yelling in my ear!" Tony shouts.

"They raided JJ's house!"

"What?"

"I said, the police raided JJ's house at 5 o clock this
morning."

"Where you at?"

"I'm in McDonald's on West Market Street."

"I'll be there in two minutes," says Tony.

Tony is close. He's in Georgia King Village. It takes him two minutes just like he said.

When Du spots the Porsche he hurries and jumps in. As soon as he gets in he lays the seat all the way back and glances around nervously like someone is after him.

"Hurry up, pull off!"

"What happened?" Tony asks.

"I didn't get the whole story yet. All I know is at 5 am; they ran up in there. I heard they blocked the streets off and everything. It was like 30 cops, narcotics force and suit and tie detectives. They even had the swat team with their riot gear on."

"Yeah? What was in there?"

"JJ fucked up Tone. We just stashed 600 grams in there yesterday, and you know all those guns were in there."

"Damn, how many?"

"He had the M-16, a Tech-9, a .45, and that little snub nose 38."

"That's enough to finish him."

"For sure," Du agrees.

"Where is E at?"

"I don't know. He's laying low. I haven't heard from him since he called me earlier and told me. He's probably down his cousin's house, down Pennington Court."

"You need to be laying low too," Tony suggests. "Do you think he'll run his mouth?"

"I don't know, that's a lot of shit. You know how the saying goes 'pressure busts pipes.' I hope not though."

"Ya'll have to hurry up and snatch him as soon as he gets a bail. Don't give him no time to think that ya'll leaving him in there. If he even get the slightest feeling that ya'll not coming to get him, he'll sing like a canary."

Du sits there with fear written all over his face.

"I'm telling you now; his bail is going to be high as hell," says Tony.

"That's the problem; we don't have a lot of cash. We bagged up 400 grams and put it out on the streets. I don't know how much he collected. We only got hold to a few thousand."

"Don't worry, I got you. I got a few dollars I can spare. Meanwhile you can hide out in my apartment. Just cool out there until we find out what's going on."

"Good looking out."

As Tony drives to his apartment Du sits there going crazy. He's scared to death. He's almost 90% sure that JJ will tell. Du doesn't want to go to jail. If he goes to jail his family will cut him off. They're totally against drug dealers.

When they pull in front of the house Tony hands Du the house key, and Du takes off up the stairs. Tony rides off. He feels sorry for Du. He can see the fear in his eyes. He doesn't really know JJ, so he can't say whether or not he will rat. All he can do is hope that JJ is a true soldier.

CHAPTER 42

Next morning

Du and JJ's last foster mother got up bright and early to meet with the bail bonds men. Du still hasn't heard anything from E. The bail bonds men said JJ's bail is 250k bond, and in order to get him they need $25,000. Du came up with 10k and Tony lent him the other 15k.

Du sits in the waiting room, while JJ's foster mother handles the paper work. She put everything in her name. They wouldn't accept her cash with out her proof of income, and her proof of address. They need to know her whereabouts just in case JJ doesn't come back to court.

Du feels much more at ease, knowing JJ is on his way home. Du didn't sleep one wink last night. He can't wait to hear what JJ has to say. He thinks he can look in JJ's eyes and pretty much tell if he told or not.

As Du paces around in the waiting room, he notices two beautiful females sitting in the back of the room. They're watching his every move.

After minutes of staring back and forth at each other, one of the females walks to the front where Du is pacing.

"Calm down honey, it will be alright." *Du stands there grinning.* **"Hi."** *She extends her hand for a handshake.* **"My name is Cathy."**

Du shakes her hand. **"I'm Du, I mean Dawud."**

"Well Dawud, do you see my friend sitting right there? She thinks you're cute and she says she just has to have you."

"Yeah?" *He's blushing.* **"Tell her to come here."**

"Tara, come here!"

As the girl walks up Du can't help but notice her beautiful bowlegs. She's stepping like a stallion. She also has a cute little round face with dimples. Du is amazed that she is interested in him.

"Dawud, this is Tara. Tara, this is Dawud."

"Dawud?" she repeats. "Don't give me your alias; give me the name your mother gave you."

"Dawud is the name my mother gave me."

"Are you Muslim?"

"Yeah, I was born Muslim, but right now I'm not practicing the way I should."

"Why not?"

"Different situations make people do certain things that may not be right, but a man gotta do what a man gotta do."

"I hear you," Tara replies.

They go on and on for about twenty minutes before JJ's foster mother comes out. Then they exchange phone numbers. For a minute Du had totally forgotten about JJ. He only had Tara on his mind.

Du dropped JJ's foster mother off at home. He then went to Tony's apartment, where he waited for Tara to call his cellular phone. She told him she had to post bail for her younger brother, and the minute she was done she would call him.

CHAPTER 43

Meanwhile, Tony and Reemie have just finished meeting with Breeze. He just bought four kilos. Breeze is killing them, and Tony isn't doing too bad himself. Tony made a profit of $12,000 off the deal. He kept $10,000 and he gave Reemie $2,000 just like he always does when he serves Breeze.

Tony is now dropping Reemie off, so he can meet with O-Drama. Over the past couple of months they have been hanging out a little more then usual. They're almost inseparable.

Tony goes to his apartment after dropping Reemie off. He has to meet Du, to find out how everything went.

When Tony walks in the apartment, Du is on the phone, blushing and smiling from ear to ear. Tony closes the door behind him.

"What's up nigga!"

"Shh," Du whispers, *as he puts one finger in the air as if he's saying wait a minute. Du talks for a few more minutes then he finally hangs up.*

"What the fuck? Were you making love on the phone?"

"Stop playing!" Du shouts.

"Who was that?"

"This girl I met at the bail bondsmen office. She bad as hell!"

"Yeah?" Tony asks. "She can't be that bad, fucking around with your ugly ass," Tony teases.

"You crazy, you wish you looked as good as me."

"Yeah alright," Tony replies. "What's up with JJ?"

"We paid the bail. He should be out tonight. Thanks again for the money."

"I told you to stop thanking me. What's up with E?"

"I just talked to him. He said, he's on his way over. He said he got hold to $9,000. He wants to know if you will get us a half a joint, and let us owe you $1,500."

"No doubt," Tony replies.

Ring, ring! Tony's phone is ringing.

"Hold up Du. Hello?"

"Tony, this is Aunt Renee." *This is Auntie, she doesn't call him Nephew anymore, and she doesn't allow him to call her Auntie either. She said those names were part of her past. Out of respect he calls her Aunt Renee now that she is all cleaned up.*

"Hey, what's up?"

"Tony, whatever you do, don't come around here. Police cars are parked on every corner. They have been driving through here all day. One of your little runners told me to call you and tell you. He said under covers have been coming through trying to buy large amounts of coke and saying nephew told them to meet them here."

"Yeah?" he slowly asks. "They asking for nephew?"

"Yes Tony, be careful baby."

After hanging up he just stands there staring at the ceiling with a confused look on his face, until the doorbell rings and brings him back to reality. Du runs straight for the door.

"Hold up!" Tony shouts. "Let me look out the window first." Tony peeks out the window. "Go ahead, it's only E."

Tony is nervous. He thought maybe the police had followed him there.

Du returns with E. Tony immediately tells them what Aunt Renee told him. Everyone stands there dumbfounded. They're sure someone is talking, but they don't know who.

CHAPTER 44

Later that evening

    The three of them wait for JJ to get out of the County Jail. They're sitting in E's jeep parked on 13th Avenue.
    After almost two hours of waiting, JJ is finally released from the side door.
    They all rise up in their seats as he approaches the jeep. Everyone pays close attention to the look on his face. They're trying to figure out did he run his mouth. JJ hops in the truck happy as he can be.
    "What up, what up?" he yells. *Everyone mumbles under their breath.* **"Yo, shit is crazy!"**
    "What happened?" E asks.
    "I don't know. The only thing I think it could be is, the night before they hit my house this cracker kept coming back and forth through the location. *(that's was what they nick named the block.)* **He kept asking for weight. I kept telling him that I didn't have weight, but he kept begging me. Then later on, I went home to get some more shit because the block was dry. When I walked out the house I saw the same cracker riding by."**
    "What kind of car was he in?" E asks.
    "A black Toyota. Tony, the whole time I was in there they kept asking me what's up with Nephew. I told them, I don't know a Nephew. I think they believed me, but they just wanted to see if I was going to change my story. You know me; I'm a real nigga. I've never told on anybody and I never will."
    I hope not, Tony thinks to himself. Tony had already planned to have him killed if he even looked like he told something, but after hearing his story, for some strange reason they all feel convinced that JJ didn't snitch.

The next morning

Reemie and Tony are on their way to meet Flaco. Tony has to pick up the half a bird he promised E and Du and he has to get his normal weekly package of two and a half kilos.

Tony has to be very careful. It's only 10 in the morning and he has already received two calls from the location letting him know the under covers have driven through.

"Shit is blazing around there!" Tony shouts. "I ain't gone lie they got a nigga a little nervous."

"Don't worry Cuzzo; just keep doing like you've been doing it and you'll be alright."

"The only reason I'm nervous is because I don't know why they keep asking for me, and who told them about me."

"Listen Cuzzo, no one person had to tell them about you. The block is grossing $125-150 thousand a week. It's no quiet way to make $150,000 a week. The streets are talking. All them cops have to do is grab one of them crack heads up and give them a bottle and they will tell everything they know. Always remember, a junkie ain't got no loyalty."

"You're right," Tony agrees. "Right now I need you more than ever." Tony admits. "We are a team, right?"

"For sure," Reemie replies.

"Well, we gotta play team ball now. You're my center, my big man on the court, you gotta hold me down. I'm the guard. I'm going to deliver. Whatever it takes for me to get that ball down the court I'm gonna get it there. Now, when I pass the ball to you, baby you gotta make it happen. You understand me?"

Reemie pauses before answering.

"Yeah."

"This is what I'm saying, I'm about to go on the low and keep my face off the scene. I'm not even coming through there.

If I'm outta sight, I'll be outta mind. I'll meet you, give you the work, and you handle it from there."

"Don't worry Cuzzo, I got you."
Tony passes Reemie his cellular phone.

"Dial this number for me, 917-563-0824. *Reemie begins dialing.* **Put my number in, hit the star button and then enter 3000."** *3000 represents three kilos. That's a half for E and Du, and two and a half for Tony.*

Shortly after that they pull up to Flaco's house.

Flaco has every thing ready so it doesn't take any time at all. Tony ran in and out.

Tony gives Reemie a half a bird to work with. This is the last they will see of each other until that's finished. Tony isn't worried about Reemie shorting him because he knows exactly how much he should bag up off of that. Tony has the shit down to a science. He bags up with a scale. He knows exactly how much each gram should make. He's going to try Reemie out for a few weeks and see how things turn out.

After dropping Reemie off, Tony took E and Du their work and he bounced. His whereabouts nobody knew. He didn't tell anyone because he doesn't trust anyone. He didn't even tell his mother where he would be. He knows that his mother, being the Christian woman she is, she won't lie, not even to protect him. Even if she wanted to lie, he's sure she'll crack under pressure. So for the next couple of weeks, or until things calm down, anybody who needs to speak to him has to call his cellular phone.

CHAPTER 45

Four months later

For the past four months things with E and Du have been real shaky. They had to change the whole operation. They rent a one-bedroom apartment in the Ivy Hill section of Newark. No one lives in it. They use the apartment as a stash house. They keep all their guns and work in there. The only people who know about the apartment are E and Du. They didn't even mention it to JJ. They're almost sure he didn't tell the cops anything but it's still a small chance that he did.

JJ didn't have a place to stay after they raided his house, so E let him move in with him and Aisha. Aisha hates the living arrangement, but this is E's way of keeping an eye on JJ.

JJ doesn't come out much. He just helps out around the house. Every now and then E let's him make a drop off to the block if he isn't around.

Du doesn't come out much either. He does whatever he needs to do on the block, and then he will go hang out with Tara. That's how he spends all of his spare time. E clowns Du all the time because he has spent everyday with her for over four months and he has never even kissed her. Du has fallen madly in love with her.

The summer has come and gone and Tony is still hiding. No one expected this to go on this long. The police haven't given up either. Just the other day they kicked in the door of Tony's old apartment. Luckily he no longer lives there. He hasn't even driven by there in months.

Tony is stressed out of his mind. He's losing weight rapidly. He's starting to look so bad that his Mom asked him is he getting high. The only thing that's going good for him is the $12,000 profit he makes off of Breeze every week.

Tony and Reemie are just meeting up. They're on 12th street, by the graveyard.

"Here goes the rest of the cash from the other day," says Reemie.

Tony met with Reemie the other day. Reemie was supposed to turn in $25,000 but instead he handed Tony $18,000 and told him the rest of the work was still on the street.

Reemie hands the money over to Tony. Tony counts it once, and then he counts it again.

"This is only $4,000."

"What is it supposed to be?"

"$7,000."

"How?" Reemie questions.

"You gave me $18,000 the other day. It was supposed to be $25,000. 25 minus 18 is seven, that's how."

"So, what do I owe you?"

"$3,000."

"Alright, I got you on the next one."

"You told me that the last time," says Tony. "Reemie, what the fuck is going on?"

"Going on with what?" Reemie asks defensively.

"You and this short shit. Every time I turn around you gotta get me on the next one, but every time I see you and O-Drama ya'll having a ball living it up."

"O ain't got shit to do with this. Leave him out of it."

"Hell no, he got a lot to do with it. Every time I turn around he at the location all up in my business."

"Your business?" Reemie chuckles. "Alright, you don't have to worry. I won't have him all up in YOUR BUSINESS anymore. You can drop me off right here, Tony. I'll walk back."

Tony, he thinks to himself. This is the first time Reemie called him Tony since he's been home.

Tony pulls over and Reemie jumps out.

"Call me when you get the new work," says Reemie, *as*

Tony pulls off. Tony doesn't like the way Reemie has been acting the past few weeks. He's always short with the money, and he has an attitude every time they see each other. Maybe he's power tripping because he knows Tony needs him. Tony really hates the fact of him being with O- Drama. Maybe Reemie is getting high, Tony thinks to himself.

Tony is on his way to see Flaco.

When Tony gets to Flaco's house, Flaco is on the stoop waiting for him. They walk up together. Once Tony gets in, he plops onto the recliner.

Flaco notices the difference; Tony spends less money each time he comes.

"What's the matter, Poppy?"

"I'm stressed out, Flaco. Ever since I let my cousin run the block everything has been going down hill for me, and the fucked up thing is the cops are still on my back. I'm thinking about walking away from all this shit."

"Fire your cousin. That's all you have to do. And as far as the police being on you, that comes with the job. They got their job, and we got ours. Don't stress over shit you can't control. You can't control the police. You have to learn to work around them."

"You right, Flaco."

Flaco hands Tony the work. "Here, one and a half. That's what you wanted, right?"

"Yeah," Tony replies. *Tony knows he should be buying more, but he knows if he buys more Reemie will mess up more.*

"What are you going to do?" Flaco asks, *while Tony is handing him the money.*

"About what?"

"About the block."

"I'm not sure yet."

"Listen, before you walk away from that block and let someone else get rich off your hard work; think about this, I'll give you a $100,000 cash for the block. How many workers do

173

you have?"

"Seven."

"Ok, I'll give you another $5,000 for each worker that you give me. Altogether that's a total of $135,000, cash!

Tony can't believe what Flaco is asking him to do. He's asking him to sell a block that doesn't even belong to him, and he also wants him to sell seven grown ass men as if he's a slave trader. Flaco is willing to pay the large amount for the block because he knows he can make his money back in no time.

"Well, what do you think?" Flaco asks.

"Let me sleep on it. I'll get back to you."

Tony leaves the apartment with that on his mind. $135,000 plus the money he has already saved. With that he can go away to school and live happily ever after. School, he thinks to himself. That's something that hasn't crossed his mind in a long time.

As Tony is driving, he thinks about Flaco. Did he make that offer because he cares about him? Or is he looking out for himself? Maybe Flaco is the one who put the cops on him; thinking that the pressure would break him and he would accept the offer, then he could have the block all to himself.

Tony is really losing his mind.

CHAPTER 46

Reemie has been calling Tony's phone all day non-stop. Tony didn't answer because he doesn't know how to tell him that their business relationship is over. Tony still loves him. He just doesn't want to do business with him anymore.

Tony has to put some work on the block, so he borrowed his friend's car. Police have never seen him in it, so they won't be expecting him to come through in it. This way he can sneak in, drop off the work and sneak back out, but to Tony's amazement the first face he sees when he drives through isn't the police. It's Reemie's.

Tony pulls alongside the curb. His little man jumps in the car, grabs the shopping bag and takes off through the alleyway of the abandoned building.

As Tony pulls off Reemie runs off the porch.

"Yo!" Tony steps on the brakes. Got damn, Tony thinks to himself. Reemie opens the passenger's door, and gets in. Tony speeds off.

"I have been calling you all motherfucking day," Reemie says aggressively.

"Oh Yeah?" I had my cell phone off."

Reemie turns towards Tony and looks him dead in the eyes. "Don't give me that bullshit. You always have your phone on."

"Nah, I'm serious!" Tony claims.

Reemie knows Tony is lying because he keeps looking away as he speaks.

"So you dropped the work off to that kid, huh?"

"Yeah, but it was just a little something though," says **Tony,** *while still looking straight ahead.*

"I told you to call me when you got it. What happened?"

"Oh, I got it late last night."
"So, why didn't you call me this morning?"
"I, I," Tony stutters. *He's running out of lies.*
"Tony cut the shit!"

There he goes with the Tony shit again, Tony thinks to himself.

"I got to keep it real with you; this business thing with us ain't working. I'm watching my money go down. I mean I love you and all, but we can't get money together," Tony explains.

"It's funny, that's the same thing I've been thinking. I didn't know how to tell you though. I'm my own man. I can't keep sitting here letting you spoon-feed me. I gotta do my own thing."

"You're right, but what is it that you want to do?" Tony asks.

Tony is hoping and praying that Reemie is not planning to do his own thing out there. If that's what he plans to do, they're going to have a major problem. Tony feels like he has been through too much to let some one come out there and do what ever they want.

Tony's heart is beating extra fast as he waits for Reemie's response.

"Well, my man I was knocked off with gave me the green light to come on his block and get money with him. He's from Little Bricks. The only catch is, I have to supply my own product." Whew! What a relief, Tony thinks.

"So you're straight than?" Tony asks.

"No, that's the problem. I'm fucked up."

"Fucked up, what about all the cash we've been making?"

"I've been spending it. I haven't saved a dime. I'm just getting home. I've been away for ten years of my life. I was living it up, trying to make up for loss time," Reemie explains.

"I feel you, but you have to save your dough. See the fucked up thing about getting fast money is; you get it fast and you spend it fast," says Tony. "Getting money is no problem, but you have to learn how to hold on to it. In this game you never know when shit

is going to go sour."

"That's true," Reemie agrees.

"So what are you trying to start out with?"

"Whatever," Reemie replies. "You don't have to hit me with nothing big. Give me something small, like an ounce. As soon as I get on my feet I'll hit you right back."

"An ounce? What the fuck can you do with an ounce?" Tony asks. Tony sits quietly for a second. "Check, I got a quarter (250 grams) left, my man from Seth Boyden was supposed to come and get it but he never showed up. I'll bring it to you later on."

"Thanks, Cuzzo." Now I'm Cuzzo again, Tony thinks to himself. "As soon as I make the money for the quarter, I'll call you. How much do you want back off of that?" Reemie asks.

"Don't worry about it, we're even."

At this time Tony is just happy to get Reemie off his team. He would have given Reemie anything he asked for. If Reemie bags up correctly he can make about $16,000 off the quarter.

"Cuzzo, just because we ain't working together, don't think I don't have your back. If you need me, don't hesitate to call. I'll still bust a nigga's ass for you. Regardless, we're still family."

Tony sucks his teeth and looks Reemie in the eyes. You think I don't know that?"

"You better know!" Reemie shouts.

Tony pulls back to the block and lets Reemie out.

"I'll call you about 2 am, so we can meet and I can give you that, alright?"

"Bet!" Reemie replies. "Later Cuzzo! I love you!" Reemie screams, as he jumps out of the car.

As Tony drives home he feels at ease. He thought Reemie would take things differently but everything worked out for the best.

CHAPTER 47

    It's now 3:30 am. Tony is late for the meeting with Reemie because he overslept. He has just arrived. He hates to make moves this late but he wants to get Reemie squared away.

    Meanwhile at E and Aisha's house, E is peeking out of the front window as Aisha's girlfriends are dropping her off.

    They went to a party and she's just getting in. E is furious. He's a jealous madman when it comes to Aisha. When they're out, he argues with anyone who looks at her. Everywhere they go he makes a fool of himself.

    As soon as the door slams behind her, he starts.

    "Where the fuck are you coming from?"

    "The Tunnel," she replies innocently.

    "The Tunnel? In New York?"

    "Yes."

    "You went all the way to New York?"

    "Yeah, that's where they wanted to go."

    "Why didn't you call me and tell me where you were going?"

    "Because I knew you wouldn't let me go," she replies, as she lowers her eyes to the floor. She's starting to get nervous.

    "So you knew I wouldn't let you go, but you went anyway, huh?"

    "E, I don't want to argue, please," she begs.

    "You should have thought about that earlier, while you was all up in niggas faces and shit." The thought of dudes trying to rap to Aisha is driving him mad.

"How many niggas did you meet tonight?" Aisha doesn't respond.

He pushes her against the wall. "I asked you a mother-fucking question!" Now he's close up on her talking to the top of her head while she holds her head down looking at the floor.

"None," she mumbles.

"Stop lying to me!"

"I'm not lying."

He snatches her pocketbook and starts to look through it. "If I find a number in here, I'm going to fuck you up!" After looking through it and finding nothing, he slams the pocketbook to the floor. "It's four in the morning, and you come walking up in here like shit alright. Four in the motherfucking morning! You weren't in no Tunnel, you probably just coming from the hotel."

Aisha looks E in the eyes. She's hurt. She can't believe he's accusing her of cheating. Aisha is a good girl and she's loyal to him. She has never given him a reason to think that. All she does is go to work, come home, and wait for him to get in, at whatever time of night that he decides to come in.

Before she can respond, E slaps her across the face. Aisha stands there holding her eye. She's shocked. He slaps her again. Now she's crying hysterically. He picks her up and slams her to the floor. "You just finished fucking? Let me smell your panties!"

Aisha can't believe this is happening. "Get the fuck off me!" she screams, while E struggles to unzip her jeans. Aisha is kicking and scratching like a wild woman.

"If you weren't fucking let me smell them!"

"Hell no!" E slaps her again. As she goes to hold her lip, E slides her jeans down to her knees. Aisha can feel her lip swelling. E tugs on her panties until he finally rips them.

Aisha starts to scream even louder. "Get the fuck off me!"

All the noise wakes JJ. He's not aware of what's going on. He runs to the living room half sleep. As he enters the room he sees E ripping Aisha's panties while she's screaming as loud as she can.

"Get this crazy motherfucker off me!"

JJ runs over and grabs E.

"Mind your business, J." He continues to slap Aisha around. Then he stands up and kicks Aisha in the ribs. Aisha is crying loud and hard. E tries to kick her again but JJ pushes him into the wall. E takes a swing at JJ. JJ ducks it and slams E onto the couch. E is embarrassed. He knows he can't beat JJ. JJ is much bigger and stronger than him. He stands up and charges JJ again. JJ scoops him and slams him again.

"Go ahead!" JJ shouts. "Cool out; stop beating on that girl like that."

E feels like JJ is trying to belittle him. He gets up again. This time he grabs his gun off his waist and aims at JJ.

Aisha screams, "E, please don't shoot him!"

E backs JJ up against the wall. "Why the fuck are you minding my business?"

JJ humbles himself. "Chill E, I didn't want you to hurt her," JJ whispers. E still has the gun aimed at him.

Aisha is begging, "Please E, stop!"

"Why the fuck are you worried about me hurting her? I take care of this motherfucker!" he shouts, as he points to Aisha with his other hand.

"Come on, E," JJ whispers.

E surprisingly smacks JJ on the chin with the gun. The impact knocks JJ off his feet. E immediately jumps on top of him.

"I'm calling the cops!" Aisha shouts.

As she's running towards the phone, E turns to her and aims the gun at her head. "Bitch, if you touch that phone, I'll blow your head off!" He then turns back to JJ and puts the gun to his forehead. Aisha stands there motionless. "J, I will kill you! Don't ever disrespect me!" E can see the fear in JJ's eyes.

JJ is his heart. He loves JJ. What is happening? He starts to feel terrible. He gets up off of JJ. He stuffs his gun back in his pants.

JJ is scared to death. He gets up slowly. He never once takes his eyes off E.

E feels terrible. He has just threatened to kill two of the people he loves the most in the world. He plops onto the couch and closes his eyes. He's crying inside.
E cries himself to sleep.

CHAPTER 48

Now that Reemie is gone Tony doesn't know what he's going to do. The $135,000 that Flaco offered him is sounding better and better each day. Tony was stuck until Du came up with a plan.

"Let me and E run the block for you."

"What about your block?" Tony asks.

"We'll just let it go. It's slow as hell anyway."

"I don't know. I'm getting tired of all the aggravation, the ducking and dodging the police, all this shit. I'm about ready to walk away from this shit."

"You can't do that Tony."

They both sit there quietly for a few seconds.

"I know a way we all can benefit from this," Du claims. "Listen, why don't you just front E and me the birds and we pay you whatever price you want for them." He looks at Tony waiting for a response.

Tony thinks about it before replying.

"That might just work. Let me see, if I front them to ya'll; will you give me $25,000 for each bird?"

"$25,000, yeah, it's on you. It's your block and your work. I have to go with what you say."

Tony starts calculating in his head. He's paying $21,000 for a bird. If he fronts it to them at $25,000, that's $4,000 profit per bird. The block is good for three birds a week. $4,000 x 3 = $12,000 profit, plus the $12,000 profit from Breeze that's $24,000 a week profit without even standing on the block. How sweet is that? Tony shakes his head up and down. "Yeah, we can do it like that."

"Are you sure?" Du asks.

"Yeah, let me go see my peoples and then we can take it

from there."

Tony has to meet with Flaco today anyway. Breeze is ready for his weekly package. Today Tony is spending more money with Flaco than he has ever spent. He's buying 6 kilos. That's three for E and Du, and three for Breeze.

Flaco doesn't have to front him the work for Breeze any more. He was only in need of his help in the beginning. After a few weeks of dealing with Breeze, Tony got his money up.

Altogether Tony is spending $126,000. Flaco will have to bring the price down today. Tony is determined to get a better price. He's sure Flaco will lower the price, because he will not want him to leave out the door with all that money.

Tony beeps Flaco and presses the code in (6000). Flaco calls him right back. He doesn't normally do that, but he wants to make sure Tony didn't make a mistake.

Once Tony gets to Flaco's apartment there are two Colombians in there with Flaco. That's his connection. They're filthy rich. Flaco told Tony that one time he went to one of their houses, and they showed him a wall full of kilos. The birds were stacked up from the floor up to the ceiling, all the way across the entire wall. Sometimes they front Flaco up to forty birds at a time. These two guys are so low keyed you would never suspect them of being drug kingpins. They look like two average, old, Colombians with salt and peppered hair. They both have on tight polyester trousers, dress shoes and tight v-neck t- shirts.

They just dropped off the new shipment of 25 birds. Flaco hands them the cash he owed from the last package and they leave the apartment.

Tony sits there staring at the kilos piled up on the coffee table. He starts calculating in his head (like he always does.) 25 birds at $21,000 a pop = $525,000. A half a million, right here in my face, Tony thinks to himself.

"Poppy! Poppy!" Tony snaps out of the thought.

"What were you thinking about? I've been calling you for the past 2 minutes."

"Oh nothing," Tony replies.

"Poppy you have to see these, they're beautiful.

"Yeah?"

Flaco cracks one open and hands Tony half. Beautiful it is. It's shiny and white just the way Tony likes them.

"Go ahead poppy, pick the six you want."

Tony is sitting there trying to figure out what he's going to say to Flaco, when Flaco interrupts his thoughts. "So did you think about my offer?" Flaco asks.

"Yeah," Tony replies immediately.

"Well, what are you going to do?"

"I thought about it but I came up with something else."

"What?"

"I'm going to let my two boys get the block. They're going to run it for me. I'm just going to provide the blow."

"Oh yeah," Flaco asks.

"Yeah, I'm going to front it to them and let them pay me when they're finished. That way I can still eat without being out there."

"Poppy, you know you can't depend on nobody to run your business for you. You should have learned that from doing business with your cousin. The next thing you know your money will be going down and down."

"No not this time, I got a plan. I have a lot of people who come to me wanting to buy work. So what I'm going to do is, start wholesaling, you know, ounces, quarters, and halves, whatever."

"Poppy, you have to be careful with that. Dealing with too many people is no good."

"I'm only going to deal with a few people," says Tony.

"Yeah, that is how it starts, before you know it a few people turn into too many people."

"Nah, I'm not going to let it get like that," Tony claims. "I only have one problem; I need a better price so I can beat out my competition. What is the best you can do for me?"

Flaco calculates in his mind before speaking.

"Come on Flaco, I'm buying six birds."

"The best price I can give you is $19,500."

"Come on, Flaco."

"That's the best I can do. I'm paying $19,000. I'm only making a half a point ($500) off of each kilo."

Tony knows he's lying because he overheard the conversation Flaco had with the Colombians. Flaco only pays $16,000 per kilo.

"$19,500 is the best I can do."

Tony doesn't respond. He's trying to hold out, hoping that Flaco will drop the price a little more.

"I tell you what." Flaco pauses. Tony waits anxiously for him to say it. "Listen, $19,500 right, but if you buy five birds I'll front you five birds."

Tony can't believe what he's hearing. That's ten kilos. If Tony moves 10 every week he can profit $45,000 a week.

He immediately accepts the offer. He counts out $97,500 out of the $126,000 he has in his bag. He hands Flaco the money. Then he packs the 10 birds and the $28,500 he has left over in his duffle bag. He dashes out of the apartment. He's so anxious to put everything in motion.

CHAPTER 49

Two months passed so fast. It's December already. They say time flies when you're having fun, and they're definitely having fun. Everyone is doing splendid. Tony goes through ten birds every week with ease. The only thing is, he dropped his price. He's not selling them for $24,000. He lowered the price to $21,500. He profits $20,000 a week. He has customers from everywhere buying weight. He even hooked up with a kid from Delaware who buys two kilos every Wednesday.

E and Du go through three a week and Breeze buys four. The rest he sells to local small time dealers, half ounces here, 200 grams there.

As for E and Du they're living large. They just bought two brand new Range Rovers. They paid cash for them. E even bought Aisha a brand new car. JJ drives it most of the time, running errands for Aisha or E. E only uses JJ as an errand boy. He no longer respects JJ. He talks down to him like he's less than a man. It seems like E doesn't have much use for him since he isn't making him money anymore.

As for Tara and Du, they're still hanging strong.

Tony hardly ever sees Reemie unless he's at Breeze's house when he drops off the package. They don't talk much because O-Drama is always around.

O-Drama is looking terrible. This has to be his all time low. It seems like the more money Breeze makes, the worse O-Drama looks. Reason being; the more Breeze makes, the more he gives O, and the more O gets, the bigger his drug habit gets.

CHAPTER 50

It's mid December. It's freezing outside, it's only like 18 degrees. Just two days ago there was a terrible snowstorm.

Du and E both have their Rovers parked on the block. They're on opposite sides of the street. E is standing by his truck discussing some business with one of the runners. You can't tell him anything. He just knows he's the shit. He has on a full-length black mink coat with the hat to match. His diamonds are so bright that, when the reflection bounces off the snow, it's enough to blind you. Du has been sitting in his Rover with the heat blasting all day as he watches the crack heads run back and forth through the alleyway. The whole time he's been sitting there he has been on the cellular phone with Tara.

E walks over to Du's truck and taps on the window. Du rolls down the window.

"Hold on, Tara," Du whispers.

"They're almost finished," says E.

"Damn, I just brought that out here not even two hours ago," Du replies. They bring out 500-dime jugs at a time.

"Shit rolling, baby!" E shouts.

"Alright, I'm going to get it," says Du.

This will be his last trip for the night. Being that they close the block early on Sundays, he's only going to bring out 100 jugs. It's already four o clock. They'll be able to finish those by 7:30. On Sunday they close shop at 7:30, but the rest of the week they're open from 10 am-10 pm.

Du talks to Tara on the phone for the entire ride to the stash house. It's a slow ride because of all the snow on the ground. Du has to take the busy streets because on the less busy streets it's

*almost impossible to get through, due to all the snow. He takes
South Orange Avenue all the way up to Sanford Ave. Then he takes
Sanford all the way across to the Ivy Hill section. As he rides
across Sanford Ave, he constantly looks in his mirrors, making
sure no police are following him there. Half way through the ride
it becomes dark outside making it harder for him to see the cars
behind him.*

*When he approaches the house he doesn't stop. He circles
the block twice to make sure no one is following him. Then he
drives through the alleyway and parks in the back yard. They
always park in the back. This way the neighbors will never suspect
that no one lives in the apartment because the cars are never in the
front.*

*As Du walks up the back stairs he notices a set of footprints
in the snow leading to the doorway. The landlord, he thinks.
The landlord always comes by to throw salt down after every
snowstorm.*

*When he sticks his key in the first door it's already open.
He then steps to the door of their apartment. He sticks the key in
the top lock first, then the bottom lock. As soon as he enters the
kitchen he reaches over to the right to turn the light on. Click,
click. The light doesn't come on. He then feels his way through to
the bathroom and reaches for the string to pull. He yanks it, but the
light still doesn't come on.*

*"What the fuck?" he blurts out. Public Service must have
cut them off, he thinks to himself. As he feels his way back to the
kitchen, he hears rumbling. He picks his pace up, looking in the
direction where he hears the noise, but the noise stops. Then he
hears footsteps coming behind him. He stumbles over the kitchen
table. As he gets closer to the door he feels someone pull the back
of his coat. He snatches away and runs to the back porch.*

"Grab him!" shouts a voice.

*"I can't see him! Come here, motherfucker. If you run, I'll
shoot."*

"Where is he?"

Du finally makes it to the back porch. He's running down the stairs. His heart is racing. He's scared. The police are in the stash house. He just knows he's going to jail. He has to get away. It's too much shit in there.

He gets to the bottom of the stairs.

"There he goes!"

"Yo he's getting away, shoot him!" says the other voice.

The words shoot him echo in Du's head causing him to run even faster.

BOOM! The first shot rings, and then BOOM! There goes another BOOM! And another. Du doesn't have time to get in his truck. They're too close behind him. As he approaches the end of the alleyway another shot rings. Boom! This one crashes into the side of his rib cage.

"Aghh!" Du cries. The wound slows him down, but he still hasn't stopped. BOOM! BOOM! The second shot hits him in the leg, causing him to stumble. When he gets to the street, he looks back. They're not behind him. He continues to limp away. As he crosses the street and jumps onto the sidewalk his leg gives out on him. He falls face first. He's determined to get up, but his leg is too heavy. He lays there helplessly. He looks to his right; about 5 feet away there is a bush. He crawls behind it, where he lays there peeking to see where the cops are. His sweatshirt and pants are covered with blood. The pain is unbearable, but right now his main concern is getting away. He has two different kinds of pain; his rib cage is pounding, while his leg is burning like hell. He lays there shivering.

He looks across the street, where he sees two men running out of the back yard. One of the men has a shopping bag in his hand. Du pulls closer to the bush, but the two men run out of his sight.

Shortly after, he sees headlights approaching. The car rides past him. Surprisingly, it isn't a cop car. It's a black station wagon. The same station wagon O-Drama drives around in.

By this time police cars are speeding through the block. The sirens are echoing all over. Du pulls his cellular out and whispers to Tara,

> *"Baby, I got shot, and I need you to come get me."*

Tara is hysterical. He told her where he was, and she was there almost instantly.

She drove him straight to the College Hospital (UMDNJ) When he arrived to the hospital they rushed him upstairs immediately.

CHAPTER 51

Du's surgery took all night. He has two broken ribs and his leg is severely damaged. The bullet shattered the bone in his leg, from his hip down to his ankle. They had to put a metal rod in his leg to replace the bone. The operation took a few hours. The doctor said he'll have a permanent limp.

Tara hung around for a few hours, and then she left. She had to inform everybody about what happened. Du's father almost lost his mind when he heard the news. E was furious, but he couldn't take it out on anyone because he didn't know who did it.

It's dinnertime at the hospital. Du is only eating the applesauce; the rest of the food looks terrible. He's in a lot of pain. The nurse just gave him some pain pills, but they haven't kicked in yet.

All morning he laid there envisioning the black station wagon riding past him. He's sure that was O-Drama's car, and if it was O, Reemie had to be with him. They will have to pay for this he continuously repeats to himself every time another pain shoots through his leg. What will Tony say when he tells him his cousin tried to kill him, Du asks himself. Maybe he shouldn't tell Tony, because he might tell him Du accused him. Maybe he'll just tell E, and they can handle it themselves. He's sure they got away with the work, that's probably what they had in the bag. There was one kilo, 2000 jugs and a .357 magnum in the house.

As Du lay there debating with himself about telling Tony. Big Muslim (his father) walks in, followed by three other Muslim brothers.

Ahh shit, Du thinks. At this moment Du wishes he were dead just so he doesn't have to face his father.

"As Salaamu Alaikum! his father greets, as he enters the room.
His father walks to the chair next to Du's bed, while the other brothers just stand there. Big Muslim stands there staring at Du. You can see pity and disgust in his eyes, as he continuously shakes his head from side to side.

Big Muslim has the whole Muslim attire on today (kufi on his head and the long over garment.) His big beard makes him look meaner than he really is.

"Walaikum as Salaam," Du returns the greeting. Du wonders what his father will say next.

"How do you feel son?"

"I'm alright," Du replies.

"Alhamdu lil lah," (praise God) says Big Muslim.
Du can't even look his father in the eyes. He feels guilty. He knows the game he's playing is wrong, but he got caught up.

"Are you in a lot of pain?"

"Yeah, major pain," Du replies.

"Just be thankful. It could have been worse. I feel blessed that you're here with me having this conversation," says Big Muslim. Du nods his head up and down, agreeing with his father. "Ibn (son) I'm going to ask you a question, and I want you to tell me the truth."

His dad pauses for a moment. Here goes the big question, Du thinks to himself, as he looks his father in the eyes. "What is it Dad?"

"What happened last night?"
Du doesn't respond at first, until his father speaks again.

"I want the truth!"

Du hates the fact of having to tell his father he got robbed at the stash house, but he has to. He can't lie to him.

"Someone tried to rob me as, I was getting away they started shooting at me."

"Where did this happen?"

"Ivy Hill," Du replies.

"What were you doing in Ivy Hill?"

Du pauses before speaking.

"That's where my stash house was."

"Where you keep your drugs at, right?" Big Muslim asks.

They all sit quietly. Big Muslim stares into Du's eyes. Du tries to look everywhere but at his father.

"Do you know who did this to you?"

Du doesn't respond

"Did you hear me? I said, do you know who did this to you?"

"Yes," Du replies.

"So I guess you want revenge, right?"

"For sure," Du whispers.

"What are you going to do to them?"

"Cause them pain, just like they caused me," Du replies.

"Let me tell you something; you need to recognize God's signs. This is a sign from God. He could have taken your life last night, but he spared you. You're so foolish that you can't see that. Don't ever forget you are a Muslim. True Muslims are not drug dealers. True Muslims are not gang bangers. Muslim means one who submits to the will of God. The game you're playing is the devil's game. God spared you once, you don't know if he'll do it again."

Big Muslim pauses for a second before speaking again.

"Dawud, get out of the game before it's too late. You can't keep living like this. You will never get into Paradise (heaven) living this lifestyle."

"Listen Ak (brother)," says the older brother. "Don't keep taking God for granted. You need to make a change right now! That is why your Aboo (father) asked us to come with him. You need to get on the right path. If you retake your Shahada (declaration of faith) Insha Allah (if God is willing) he will forgive you for your past sins."

They all sit quietly.

"Will you do it?" Big Muslim asks. Du hesitates before speaking.

"Yes."

"You know if you do this, all your past sins will be forgiven Insha Allah, but you can't go back doing the same things all over again," Big Muslim explains.

"I know," Du replies.

"Are you ready?" the older brother asks.

"Yes, Du replies.

"Repeat after me," the older brother instructs. "Ash hadu an la ilaha ill Allah."

"Ash hadu an la ilaha ill Allah, Du repeats.

"Wa ash hadu anna Muhammadar Rasul Allah," the older brother says slowly.

"Wa ash hadu anna Muhammadar Rasul Allah," Du repeats.

    Translated that means there is none worthy of worship but Allah and Muhammad is the messenger of Allah. That is what you have to say in order to become a Muslim. The Muslims believe when you state this you are free of your past sins. You start over with a clean slate.

    "Ak, now please live the rest of your life like a true Muslim. No more guns, and no more drugs, and Insha Allah (if God is willing) you will be forgiven for your sins," says the older brother.

    Their speech is really getting to him. As he sits there staring at the ceiling, there comes a knock at the door. It's the nurse telling them visiting hours are now over.

    As Du's father and the other brothers walk out the door, they all scream, "As Salaamu Alaikum!"

CHAPTER 52

Three days have passed. Du is still in the hospital. He isn't in as much pain. He's just bored to death. All day long all he does is read his Quran. Du has made up his mind; he's going to change his life around. He knows it will be a struggle but he's determined to do it.

At this time E and Tara are at the front desk trying to get visitors passes. The receptionist told them Du has visitor restrictions. Du's father instructed the hospital not to let any visitors up because he fears for his son's life, plus he figured the time alone would help Du get his mind right.

"Damn, we can't even see him!" E shouts, as he holds the door for Tara to exit.

Tara is looking awesome today. She's wearing a short fox jacket. It barely covers her tiny waist, revealing her big hips. Her tight jeans fit her bowlegs perfectly.

As they approach E's Rover he opens the door for her and lets her in first. He then walks to his side, climbs in, and pulls off.

Tara doesn't say much. She only answers what E asks her. She only gives one-word answers, yes or no.

E continuously takes peeks at her. She's beautiful. How the hell did Du luck up and get one like this, he asks himself. E decides to start a conversation, just to break the silence.

"I know you can't wait for Du to come home, right?"

"Yes," she answers briefly.

"Me too," E agrees. "That's my little man." He's intentionally down playing Du. "It hurts me to know my little man is laid up in the hospital all hurt up and shit. I raised that kid. Did he tell you that?"

"No, he didn't," she replies. Tara is wondering why E thinks Du would tell her that.

"Yeah, I taught him everything he knows." He further belittles Du. "Without me, Du would be nothing. That block, I got it rocking. All Du has to do is sit back while I get us rich."

E is bragging up a storm. Everything he's saying is I, I, I. E's plan is to downplay Du and blow himself up, so Tara will think he's really the man. Everyone knows that girls are E's weakness, but never has he stooped this low.

"Tara, how a motherfucker like Du get a pretty girl like you?" She blushes. "I mean I don't judge niggas and Du my man but he ain't the most attractive motherfucker. You are so pretty. I know you have noticed how I stare at you every time we are around each other."

"No, I didn't," she answers modestly.

E is on a roll now.

"Ever since Du first introduced me to you, I asked myself, damn, why couldn't I have met her first?"

"Yeah?" she asks sarcastically.

"Yeah, word up. I was hoping ya'll didn't work out; so then maybe I could have a chance."

"What made you think I would get down like that?" Tara asks.

"I was hoping you would," E replies.

"Turn right here," she instructs.

As E pulls up in front of the Colonnades across from Branch Brook Park he pops the big question.

"I know this sounds fucked up, but I have to ask you anyway."

"What?" she asks.

"If I give you my number will you call me? This is between us. You don't have to tell Du."

"Why shouldn't I tell him?" she asks, with a devilish smirk on her face. The look in her eyes tell E she's willing to play.

"It could just be between us," E suggests.

"How do I know you're not going to tell?" Tara asks.

"I don't kiss and tell, plus do you think I would want my man to know I was kicking it to his girl?"

E begins to write his number down. He hands it to her and she reaches down to grab it.

"I don't know about this, I have to think about it."

As she opens the door and sticks her right leg out, he grabs her by her belt and pulls her back to the seat. When she turns to look at him his face is right there, his lips are puckered up. He kisses her. He thought she would pull away, but instead she initiated the kiss by sticking her tongue in his mouth and teasing his tongue with hers. After the breathtaking kiss, she pulls away, while looking him directly in the eyes. "Du is going to kill us," she says, with a look of guilt on her face.

As she walks away, E watches her ass jiggle all the way up the stairs. Not only did E push up on his best friend's girl, he has just tongue kissed her. For a quick second he feels guilty, but his lust for her overpowers his love for his best friend.

CHAPTER 53

Tony has been driving Du's Rover ever since Du went in the hospital. He can't drive the Porsche because of all the snow. Today he's going to park the Rover and drive his van because he has a lot of moves to make. He doesn't want to get Du's truck hot with the police, plus Du doesn't have a stash spot in his truck.

Tony is getting close to the block where he parked the van. As he turns the corner onto Chancellor Ave., he begins looking for it. He drives all the way to the end of the block but he still doesn't see the van. Damn, I thought I parked right here, he thinks to himself. He then busts a U-turn and drives slowly through the block. He gets all the way to the end, yet he still doesn't see the van. He looks up at the street signs; he reads 'No parking Wednesday between 9-4'. "They must have towed my shit," Tony blurts out. Tony is pissed off. Everything is going haywire. First the shit with Du, now the van is gone and on top on that the police came through the 'location' with his picture, earlier this morning. Tony is tired of all the madness.

At this exact moment somewhere on Hawthorne Ave., O-Drama lifts the cocaine filled bill up to his nose. He takes a big sniff. Before he can blink his eyes he takes another sniff. This sniff is even bigger than the first one. He twitches his nose and passes the bill to the driver. The driver begins sniffing from the bill.

The man in the driver's seat is Reemie, and the car they're in is Tony's. They stole his van earlier this morning. That's the reason Tony can't find it. They have been driving around all morning getting high. Right now they are both zooted out of their minds.

*"We out," says Reemie. Before he pulls off he folds the bill and tucks it in his pocket. He picks up his cellular phone and starts dialing. He presses the numbers, 917-563-0824. When the phone beeps, he presses * 3000 then he hangs up. After hanging up he speeds off.*

Reemie's eyes are bloodshot red and his nose is numb from all the sniffing he has done.

They're on their way to Flaco's house.

It only takes them a matter of minutes to get there. When they get to the house, Reemie, parks in the alleyway just like Tony always does.

Flaco doesn't wait for the bell to ring; he saw the van pull up in the alleyway. He immediately runs down the stairs, and opens the door. He thinks it's Tony so he leaves the door opened for him. Instead Reemie comes up by himself.

When Reemie gets up the stairs, Flaco's apartment door is open. He walks right in. Flaco is startled, because he expected Tony.

"Where is Tony?" Flaco asks nervously.

"He's on his way up. He was on the phone discussing some business."

Reemie has a shopping bag in his hand.

"Have a seat," says Flaco.

Reemie sits in the chair and places the bag on top of his lap. Flaco doesn't like the looks of this. He knows who Reemie is, but never has he been in the apartment.

"This motherfucker is taking forever," says Reemie.

Then comes the knock on the door, knock, knock. Flaco is now feeling relieved. He runs to the door, unlocks it and opens it. To his surprise, it's not Tony. It's a chrome .45 aimed at his head. "Back up come esta!" O-Drama shouts, while grabbing Flaco's neck and pushing him in the apartment.

Reemie runs over and locks the door.

O-Drama has the gun aimed at Flaco. "What's going on, Poppy?" Flaco asks.

"Shut the fuck up como esta!" O shouts. Reemie starts ransacking the apartment.

"Come esta, where the birds at?" O asks.
Flaco doesn't answer. Reemie walks over to Flaco, and sticks his gun in Flaco's mouth. "Where are the birds? You got a safe in here?"

"Yes," Flaco replies instantly. He fears for his life.
"Let's make it happen!" Reemie shouts.
Flaco gets up and starts to lead them to the bedroom.

O has Flaco by the arm while the other hand holds the gun against Flaco's back.

"I don't want no funny business," says Reemie.
Once they enter the bedroom, Flaco walks straight to the closet.

"Wait; let me open it," Reemie demands.
He aims his gun at the closet, and quickly pulls the door open; only clothes are visible.

"Where the fuck is the safe?" O asks.
Flaco starts pulling clothes off the top shelf. After all the clothes are pulled down they finally see the safe.

"Open it!" Reemie screams.
Flaco starts turning the dial on the safe. He's so nervous he can't remember the combination. He tries it three times and it still won't open.

O is starting to believe that Flaco is stalling purposely. He smacks Flaco over the head with the butt of the gun.

"Aghh! Ok ok, I'll get it open," Flaco cries.
Flaco, turns it again, and CLICK. It opens. There they are. Five kilo's are stacked up in there.

Reemie grabs the five birds and lay them on the bed.
"Where the cash at?" O screams.
"There is no money, that's it," Flaco cries.
Reemie dumps the contents from his bag. It's nothing but newspaper. He used the newspaper to fill the bag so Flaco would think he had money in there.

He fills the bag with the five kilos. Reemie fumbles inside the stack of newspaper, and pulls out some rope and duct tape.

"Come here como estas, turn around."

Flaco turns around like Reemie instructed him to. Reemie starts tying the rope around his wrist behind his back. Then he bends down and ties the rope around his ankles.

"I'm going to ask you one more time, where is the cash?" O says furiously.

"I swear there is no cash. My connection, he picked it up already."

O grabs the duct tape and wraps the tape from Flaco's mouth to the back of his head, and then he pushes him.

Flaco falls face first onto the bed.

"Come on!" says O, as he runs out of the bedroom. Reemie follows him.

O reaches to open the living room door, "Hold up!" Reemie shouts. He then runs back into the bedroom, BOOM! BOOM!

CHAPTER 54

The next morning Tony found his van parked on Prince Street parked by the projects. Reemie and O left it there, after the robbery. When Tony found it the only thing wrong was the door lock was out and the ignition was tore up. He knew someone stole it but never did it cross his mind that it was his cousin. He didn't hear about Flaco yet. He still has two kilo's to move before he has to meet with Flaco.

E and Tony are riding in E's Rover. They're on their way to see Du in the hospital. E talked Big Muslim into putting their names on the family list. They're both anxious to see him and hear what happened. They're totally in the dark because Du didn't tell anyone but his father the details of the incident. Tara doesn't even know the story. Du never tells her anything about his street business. His motto is the less she knows, the less she can tell if she's put under pressure.

They park on Bergen St. because the parking lot is full.

As they walk to the hospital's entrance E says, "after we leave from here I need you to get the other bird for me. I have to put the work on the street." E has already told Tony how he's going to make up for the loss of the kilo that was stolen out the house. He has given Tony everything he owed him except $7,000. He's going to pay that off with the profit from the kilo Tony is about to give him.

When they step out the elevator both of them become nervous. They don't know what to expect.

E knocks on the door. Knock, knock.

"Come in!" Du shouts.

They both enter. They're shocked to see Du sitting in the chair reading. They expected him to be laying there with tubes up *his nose.*

"What up?" Du screams. His eyes light up instantly. He sets his Quran on the nightstand.

"What's up?" they reply, as they walk over to him. E shakes Du's hand first, and then Tony walks over and hugs him.

"Where did you get hit?" Tony asks.

"My ribs and my leg," Du replies. "They had to put a metal rod in it. The doctor said I'll walk with a permanent limp."

"Damn," says E. "Are you in a lot of pain?"

"No, not now. The other day I was. I was in here crying like a baby." They all laugh.

"So how did it happen?" E asks.

Du begins telling the story word for word. He goes into every little detail.

"Did they have on masks?" Tony asks.

"No."

"So, you saw their faces?"

"No it was too dark," Du replies. Du sees it coming. He doesn't want to tell Tony what he saw but he has to. He wants them to be on point just in case they make a move on them.

"So you couldn't see anything? Who did it look like it could be?" Tony asks.

Du takes a deep breath and blurts out, "I know who it was."

"You do?" Tony asks. "Who?"

"While I was hiding in the bushes two niggas ran out. I couldn't see their faces because they ran up the street, and then I heard a car start up. The car came right past me."

"What kind of car?" E asks.

"A black station wagon."

E and Tony are trying to figure out who drives a black station wagon.

"It was O-Drama's car," says Du.

"Get the fuck out of here!" E shouts.

"Are you sure?" Tony asks.

"I'm positive, that was the car. The descriptions fit Reemie

and O."

    Tony wants to defend his cousin but he can't. Deep down inside he knows Reemie is capable of doing this.

    They all sit quietly.

    "Them slimy ass niggas!" E shouts. "This shit can't go like this. Somebody has to pay. Tony, I know that's your cousin but he crossed the line. Something has to give." E goes on and on, while Tony just listens. He can't say anything because E is totally right. But Tony also knows E won't hurt a fly. He's all mouth. He isn't going to do anything to anybody.

    For the rest of the visit Tony sits quietly. He doesn't know what to do. Reemie is his first cousin. Maybe it wasn't their car. Maybe it was one just like it, he foolishly tries to make his self believe. Who is next? Will they come after him? Nah, Reemie knows Aunt Renee will kill him. These are just some of the thoughts that are running through Tony's mind.

    E asked Du how he wanted to handle the situation. Du told him he wasn't going to do anything. He also told him he was done, out of the game, finished. E is upset. His man has turned pussy. E knows when a man is put under a situation like this, only one of two things happens. Either he develops an "I'm going all out attitude" or he folds. Du is folding.

    "So you're going to let these punk motherfuckers shoot you, and you're not going to do shit? I don't believe this shit! Du, you can't quit now, you're a soldier. You got wounded in the line of duty, that's part of the game. Get up, lace your boots, accept your purple heart and get on front line!"

    "I promised my father I would let it go," Du explains.

    "Alright! Alright!" E shouts. "You can let it go, but I'm not!" He storms out of the room. "Come on Tony!"

    Tony gets up and hugs Du. He feels like it's his fault. They were all linked together on the strength of him. They always told Tony not to trust those guys.

    Tony walks to the door with his head down.

    E's mouth has been shut for the whole ride. He knows not to say too much. After all Reemie is Tony's first cousin. Tony is quiet because he doesn't know what to say. Ring! Ring! E's phone rings.

"Yo!" he answers.

"Hello E." says the voice. It's Tara.

E's mad face turns into a smile. "What's up baby?" he asks, as he peeks at Tony.

"Are we still on for tonight?" Tara asks.

"For sure!" E replies. "I have to put some work on the block, and then I'm coming to get you."

He just told Tara all of his business. This isn't the first time. Every time he talks to her he tells her something that he shouldn't have. That's his way of making himself look like a big man.

"Let me hit you back in a little while," E insists. He rushes her off the phone because he feels guilty knowing that this is Du's girl. He feels like Tony knows but Tony never suspected anything. He thought E was talking to Aisha.

E takes Tony to get the bird. After that he drops him off immediately. E has to hurry he has a hot date tonight.

CHAPTER 55

Four days have passed. Tony has finally finished the work he had. Things have slowed down a bit because Tony barely comes through the area.

Breeze hasn't called in days. Tony has already come to the conclusion that he isn't going to deal with him. He doesn't trust any of them now. It's odd; normally Breeze would have called by now. Maybe he's working off the kilo Reemie took from the house, thinks Tony. He has to figure out a way to find out if it's true.

Tony is on his way to meet Flaco. He beeped him twenty minutes ago. Now he's on the road.

Before he gets to Flaco's block, his phone rings. It's his man from Delaware. He said he's an hour and a half away. He's coming to get his normal two pies. Tony has to hurry. He can't waste time chatting with Flaco.

He pulls up in the alleyway and jumps out. When he reaches to ring the bell he takes notice that the door is open. He goes in. This is unusual.

When he gets to Flaco's door, it's quiet. He doesn't hear the T.V. or anything.

He twists the doorknob and it opens right up. He cracks the door and peeks in. It's empty. What used to be a living room is now a big empty room. He walks in the apartment and it looks as if no one has ever lived here. Tony stands in the middle of the floor, lost. Where the hell is Flaco? Did he move without telling me, Tony asks himself. Tony doesn't think he would do that, besides he owes Flaco nearly $100,000.

Tony hears footsteps. He turns around. An old man enters the apartment.

"Are you looking for someone, son?" Tony recognizes him. He's the superintendent of the building.

"Yes sir, I'm looking for my boy, you know, the Spanish boy." The old man's face drops.

"You didn't hear?"

"Hear what?"

"I'm sorry to tell you, your buddy is dead."

"Dead?"

"Yeah dead! I found his body up here a couple of nights ago. He was lying in the bed tied up. When I found him, he had two bullet holes in his head. The police said it had to be a robbery, or a drug deal or something. Did you know your friend was a fugitive? He was a big time drug dealer," says the old man, as they walk down the stairs.

"Yeah?" Tony asks, acting surprise.

This is the worse news Tony has ever heard. This has to be Reemie's work. But how, he asks himself. Then he envisions the couple of times he took Reemie with him. Tony now realizes that they're on a mission.

He hurries up and hops in the van. There he is; sitting with $97,500 of his own buy money, and the $97,500 he owed Flaco. That's close to $200,000 buy money with no connect, and his man is on his way up to get two pies. That has to wait. More important than that, he has to call E and tell him. He wants to warn him, because for some reason he thinks E will be next. He isn't worried about himself because he knows Reemie doesn't know where to find him.

E and Tara are in Short Hills Mall shopping. E has been spending a lot of time with her. She barely goes to see Du in the hospital. She told E that Dawud (he doesn't like to be called Du anymore) isn't the same, all he talks about is religion, and how he wants her to become Muslim, so he can marry her. She told him that she isn't ready to make that commitment.

Tony calls E while he's shopping. He tells him about Flaco.

He also tells him to stay out of sight until they found out what's going on.

E cursed Tony out on the phone; he told Tony it's all his fault for doing business with those guys. Again, Tony just listened because it really is his fault. E and Du never liked or trusted those guys, but Tony's greed made him do business with them anyway.

After they hung up, E called JJ and told him to meet him on Clinton Ave. He dropped Tara off. E didn't want to go home because he knew Breeze knew where him and his sister Aisha lived. When JJ arrived E updated him on what was going on. He told JJ that he wouldn't be home for a few nights, because Breeze might send Reemie and O there. He then gave JJ $500 and told him to find a hotel to stay in. He didn't want anything to happen to JJ either, but most of all he doesn't trust him and Aisha alone in the house together all night.

The next three days no one came out. They all communicated through their phones. JJ is staying at the Days Inn on Routes 1 and 9. Tony is staying wherever it is that he stays. E is staying at Tara's house. He has Aisha fooled. He told her that him and JJ had to go to Virginia to handle some business.

In the two nights E spent with Tara, she learned so much about him. He gave her the run down of his life, from birth to present. He told her everything from the price he paid for kilos to how many he moved a week. He ran his mouth all day, and night. He even told her about Flaco getting murdered. That's the kind of guy he is, anything to make him look like a big man.

CHAPTER 56

It's 12:30 in the morning. It's pitch black outside. No one is on the streets. E has been sitting on the abandoned porch, in the middle of the block for two hours. He's freezing. He sits in the corner protecting himself from the wind. It's so dark on the porch, you can walk right past and you won't see him.

JJ is parked on the other end of the block in E's Range Rover. They're waiting for O-drama to come home. Someone gave E a tip. They told him that O comes home every night at 10:30. He is already two hours late.

It's a one-way street, so he has to pass JJ in order to get to his house. E doesn't really want to do this, but he knows he has to. He knows if he doesn't get O, they will get him next. They already shot Du. They killed Flaco. He hates to think about what they will do to him.

It's now 12:50. E is starting to get tired. He dozes off. Ring! Ring! The phone wakes him. "What up?"

"Here he comes!" JJ shouts.

E stands up and watches as the car pulls up. They're in Breeze's car (The black 850 BMW).

As the car gets closer, E prepares himself. He puts his mask on and pulls his gun out. He's carrying an Uzi. He has never shot it before, but how can he miss? He has a special clip attached to the gun. A banana clip is what they call it. It holds 60 bullets.

The closer the car gets, the harder E's heart pounds. He's a nervous wreck right now. His palms are sweating, and his hands are shaking.

Here they are. As they park in front of the house next door, E jumps off the porch into the alleyway that separates O's house

from the abandoned house. They don't see him. E creeps along
side the house.

They turn the lights off.

Now E is waiting for O to get out. The passenger door flies
open. E is so anxious that he disregards the entire plan. Before
O can put a foot on the ground, E runs out of the alleyway Boc!
Boc! Boc! Boc! Boc! He fires five shots, hitting nothing. Breeze
is startled. He steps on the gas and speeds off, while O closes the
door. Breeze is so busy looking back that he doesn't see the parked
car in front of him. Smack! He collides into the back of the parked
car. E chases behind the car. Breeze then backs up off the car
and starts driving up the street. The accident slows Breeze down,
causing E to be even closer to the car. Boc! Boc! Boc! Boc! Boc!
Boc! Boc! Boc! Boc! Boc! Boc! Boc! He recklessly fires twelve
shots at the car as it gets close to the corner. The car is almost
out of E's sight but he can see that the car is going out of control.
Instead of going straight, the car is going in the direction of the
sidewalk. Then Smack! They crash into the corner store. E runs
up the street. As he nears the corner, he can hear the horn blowing,
not like beep beep it's constantly blowing like (beeeeeeeeeeeee).

He stands close to the car. Boc! Boc! Boc! Boc! He fires
four more times. To his surprise Breeze is already hit. He's laying
there with his head resting on the steering wheel. He's dead. One
of the lucky shots must have hit him, causing the car to go out of
control. E runs to the passenger side of the car, the door is wide
open but O isn't in there. E glances around. He sees a trail of
blood leading under the car. E points the Uzi under the car and
kneels down. There lays O. He's hiding. E grabs him by the leg
and drags him from under the car. The blood is gushing from his
mouth. He lies there gagging and holding his throat. It looks like
he's having a seizure. He's been hit in the neck and the back.

As E stands over him, he thinks about Du. He then squeezes
six times rapidly. Boc! Boc! Boc! Boc! Boc! Boc!

That does it. O's hand falls to the ground. He stops
gagging. His eyes close and his head leans over to the side. JJ

pulls up. He slams on the brakes. Screech!

"Get in!" JJ shouts, as he leans over to open the passenger door for E. E still in shock, runs to the passenger side and jumps in.

The police sirens are getting closer.

As JJ drives off, E sits there with his eyes wide open in a daze. He still has the gun glued to his hand. He's in total shock. It will take some time for him to realize what he just done. Not only did he kill O-Drama; he just murdered his girlfriend's brother.

CHAPTER 57

JJ spent the night in the Days Inn, the same place he has been for the past few nights. E stayed at Tara's. E told Tara everything. He bragged on and on, about how he murdered O and Breeze.

JJ and E are out and on the road. They're on their way to Don's Diner in Irvington, for breakfast.

E is in the middle of bragging about the shooting. He boasts about how good his aim was. Ring! Ring! "Hello," E answers.

"E," says Aisha. She's sniffling and crying.

"What's up Eesh?" he asks, as if he doesn't know what she's about to say. He already planned how he was going to perform when she called.

"Somebody killed my brother!" she cries.

"Your brother?" he asks, as he nudges JJ with his elbow. "When?"

"Sometime last night," she replies. "Where are you?"

"I'm on my way home," E replies. "Right now I'm coming through Maryland."

"Please hurry up I need you," Aisha begs.

"I'll be right there, baby."

They hang up.

"Fuck that motherfucker!" E shouts.

"For real!" JJ agrees.

They proceed to the diner. After sitting there eating and talking for two hours, they leave. Aisha is expecting them.

They walk in the house. It's a wreck. E looks everywhere for her. He hears the water running in the bathroom, he stops and peeks in. There she is sitting on the floor in between the sink and the tub. She looks a mess. She has nothing but her panties on. Her hair is wild, and she looks like a mad woman. E quickly runs over to her. He covers her with a towel as he hugs her and tries to comfort her. JJ just watches.

CHAPTER 58

E hasn't spoken to Tara all day. He can't get away from Aisha. He's scared to leave her alone. He doesn't know what she will do. Him and JJ both slept there overnight.

E wakes up and looks at the clock; it reads 5:00 am. He crawls out of the bed. He's on his way to the bathroom to take a leak. He stumbles through the hall, with his eyes half open. While he stands there pissing he hears a loud strange noise. Boom! Then he hears something crash onto the floor, followed by lots of footsteps. Before he can figure out what's going on he hears.

"Freeze!" He looks at the doorway. The detective has his gun aimed at him. "Turn around, and put your hands on your head!" E does exactly what the detective instructed him to do.

The detective cuffs him and drags him into the living room. JJ is already in there. They sit them on opposite sides of the room. They have Aisha in the kitchen trying to calm her down, by telling her she doesn't have anything to worry about.

The cops then identify themselves. They are here to get JJ. He jumped bail. He never went back to court for the house raid. The police escort JJ out the house in his sweat pants and socks, no shirt. After putting JJ in the car, the other four cops walk over to E and snatch him up.

"Come on!"

"Where?" E questions.

They never replied, they just pushed him out the door. E was so embarrassed. They brought him out the house with his boxers on. The neighbors stared as he begged them to let him put his pants on. The whole ride he asked the detectives, why they were taking him.

CHAPTER 59

Five days have passed and E still doesn't know why he's locked up. They haven't even let him make a phone call. He's not in the County Jail. He's Downtown in the Gateway building, by Penn Station. E is in the cell alone. He has come to the conclusion that they found out about the murder.

While sitting there worrying, a detective opens his cell and snatches him to his feet.

"Get up!"

"Where are we going?"

The detective drags E into a tiny room. "Have a seat," the detective says, as he points to the small table and two chairs. "Somebody wants to speak with you."

E is still handcuffed, with only his boxers on. His back is facing the door.

Who are they bringing in here, E asks himself. After five minutes of trying to figure out who could be there to speak to him. The door opens. E hears footsteps. They sound like women's footsteps.

He looks up. He exhales. What a relief, it's Tara. She doesn't say anything to him, she just looks at him.

Then the detective speaks. "Eric Jackson (that's E's government name) I want you to meet Federal Agent, Tawana Jenkins."

When E hears those words he wants to faint.

Tara then smiles and says, "Hi, Eric, I mean E."

"You're a fed?" E foolishly asks.

She nods her head up and down while smiling at him.

"You stinking bitch!" he yells, as he jumps from the

*seat. The detective slaps him. "Sit down, you stupid
motherfucker!"*

*Tara laughs even harder. She then pulls a small tape
recorder out of her pocket, and starts pressing buttons.*

*E feels like an idiot as he sits there listening to every
conversation him and Tara ever had, starting with the very first one,
the day him and Tara went to see Du in the hospital. He listens to
stories he told about drugs, and murder, with descriptive details.*

CHAPTER 60

The next morning

They're dragging E to court. His mother is in the courtroom waiting for him.

They call his name, as he walks into the courtroom. He has on a tight orange jumpsuit and some slippers. He sits next to his attorney. The prosecutors bring up all the evidence they have against him; all the kilos he has sold and everything. It's very little that they don't know. The things they didn't know about, they soon found out, after Tara (Federal agent Tawana Jenkins) replayed the tape.

Then he hears the prosecutor say, "I want to bring out my witness." Witness, what witness, E thinks to himself.

His heart stops beating when he sees JJ standing there with his hand on the Bible swearing in. E can't believe his ears. JJ is telling everything. His little man, his main man, Mr. I'm a true soldier, on the stand singing like Michael Jackson.

The judge sentences E to 60 years. They're charging him with double homicide, and kingpin charges.

JJ made a deal with them. They promised to downgrade his charge if he testified on E. He'll only have to do three or four months in a correctional facility, probably, Annandale. Then he'll finish up his time in a 'half way house', where he will be able to go out all day but he'll have to be back in at night. E on the other hand, will be 82 years old if he makes it out.

Later that evening

E calls his mother. He tells her not to worry about him

because he will be alright. His mother cried the whole time they were on the phone. Before they hang up, he asks his mother to call Aisha on the three way. His mother refuses.

"Why not?" he asks.

"Baby, I got some bad news," Mom claims.

"Let me have it."

Things can't get any worse than they already are, he figures. But things did get worse. E's mom told him that after they released JJ from the courtroom, Aisha was outside the building. When JJ came out, Aisha ran over to him, hugged and kissed him in celebration.

E is crushed. He's hoping this isn't true. He isn't calling his mother a liar, but he just hates to believe that they were messing around, all the while.

He decides to call her on his own. E places the collect call to the house. He can't wait for her to answer the phone, so he can ask her if what his mom said is true. Maybe she had mistaken someone else for Aisha.

As the phone rings, he prays silently. God please let her tell me she was at work today. Please. He begs. The phone picks up, Aisha answers.

"Hello!"

"Hello, you have a collect call from Essex County Jail, inmate please state your name."

"E!" he shouts.

"Do you accept?" the operator asks.

"Hell no!" screams a male voice, before hanging up. Click.

It was JJ. His mom was right. JJ had not only testified on E, but on top of that he stole the only girl E had ever loved.

CHAPTER 61

Things are critical now. Du has been shot up. Flaco got murdered. O and Breeze were found dead. The feds had E, and JJ testified. On top of that, the police are getting closer and closer to Tony. That's too much pressure for one man to handle. He has to get away. He decides to go to North Carolina. He has family there. He'll hide there until his paperwork goes through so he can go away to school.

He has all his clothes packed in the Porsche. All he has to do is, go to his mom's house, tell her good bye, pick up his money and he's on his way to North Carolina.

"Baby, I hate to see you go away, but I'd rather you go there, than to see you go to jail or get killed," she says softly.

"Don't worry Ma, one day all this will just be a memory, and I'll just be plain old Tony again."

"I hope so," she says, as she hugs and squeezes him tightly. "Tony, I have one question for you."

"Yes Ma?"

"Do you remember some time ago, when I found out about you dealing drugs, I asked you what it was you wanted?"

"Yeah, I remember," Tony admits.

"Do you remember what your reply was?"

"No, what was it?" Tony asks.

"You told me all you wanted was to be happy. I look at you now almost two years later. You got everything, fancy cars, expensive jewelry, fur coats and lots of money. Are you happy yet?"

Tony doesn't answer. He thinks about it. The reality of it is, he was happier back then, when he was catching the bus to and from work. He can't admit that to his mom though.

Everything was so simple back then, no pressure. He didn't have to duck and dodge the police, and most of all he didn't have to carry guns to protect his money because he didn't have any money to protect. One thing the game taught Tony is; there is no love on the streets. People scream "I Love You" all day long, just like saying hi and bye. I LOVE YOU. I LOVE YOU. But the reality is, everything about the streets is temporary. When you're living the street life you're temporary because if you get caught, it's over you're gone. The streets bring you temporary friends, temporary love, temporary money and most of all temporary happiness.

Tony hugs his mother one more time before he walks out the door.

"Ma, I'll call you as soon as I get there!" he yells, as he hops in his car.

Now all he has to do is pick up his money and he's North Carolina bound.

The traffic is moving so slow on the Garden State Parkway. It's bumper to bumper. He must have sat in traffic for over forty-five minutes, before deciding to get off at the next exit, and drive through the streets. He figures that will be quicker.

He gets off at the Irvington exit and takes Springfield Avenue all the way up to Union. It doesn't take him anytime at all. He turns the corner and bingo he's there.

He parks in the back, and runs through the alleyway. He runs up the front stairs. He opens the door, skips to the back room, and grabs the duffle bag, which is filled with money (his entire savings.) He opens it to make sure the stacks are in place. Then he dashes out the door. He locks the door behind him. As he turns around he takes notice of the hallway door slowly opening. A shadow appears in the doorway. To his surprise, it's Reemie. They startle each other. Reemie didn't know Tony was there and Tony didn't know Reemie knew where to find him.

They stand there staring at each other. Neither of them are blinking. Then simultaneously they draw their guns, and aim at each other.

Two guns. Two cousins. Same bloodline. Different intentions.

Reemie's eyes are bloodshot red. He's as high as a kite. He looks Tony dead in the eyes. He bites down on his top lip, as he holds the gun to Tony's head.

Tony stands there with tears rolling down his face. His hands tremble as he holds the gun to Reemie's head. He was so close; five minutes later Reemie would have missed him.

Reemie is thinking (I can kill him right now, and take the bag of money. No one would ever know. This nigga ain't going to pull the trigger, he ain't built like that. Look at him, he crying like a bitch, shaking like a leaf, he's scared to death.)

Tony is thinking (I don't want to kill him, this is my Aunt's only son. But if I don't kill him, he's going to kill me. I could just pull the trigger, and no one would ever know.)

They stand there face to face.

Silence fills the air.

Then **(BOOM!!!!!!!)**

The one shot echoes through the entire building.

One lays there dead, and the other one makes it out.

No one would ever know. This is one secret the streets will never tell.

Acknowledgements

First and foremost I would like to thank GOD for directing me toward "MY EXIT."

Secondly I would like to thank everyone who took the time out to read this book.

My main purpose in writing this book was to give people a real sense of the street.

This is just some of the madness, that's happening in every ghetto all over the world.

While some of you maybe fortunate enough to only pass through the ghetto, using the local newspaper as your link to the streets.

There are others who are stuck in the ghetto; living their lives behind the scenes of the articles you read.

Some are there by choice, while others are there by force.

Special thanks to Mom dukes for being there and never turning her back on me. I truly apologize for all the tears and heartache I caused you. I love you. You have your hands full Reggie.

Dad, I hope y'all feeling me out there in Tennessee.

I would also like to thank my beautiful wife "Charo" for her support. The book is finally finished. Now you can get a full night's sleep. Thanks for everything. I love you.

To my brother T, and my cousins: Cuz, Markel, Jameel, Robert, and Tariq. Be patient and stay focused, I promise I'll do my best to get us out of the hood.

To my baby sister, Chantel, my daughter Fajr, my nephew Aziz, and my little cousins Saraya, Shanequa, Davonne, Javonne, and Kyon, I love ya'll. I hope and pray that this book is the closest ya'll get to the game.

Naimah and Danielle keep up the good work. Keep striving; I know you both will be successful.

Doris, Malik, Nise, Gena, Jeff, Toni, Uncle Jameel, Debbie, Tyese, Kamillah, Monroe, Ingrid, Dennis, James Danzey, what up!!

Granny those prayers have definitely protected me. I love you. Grandaddy unlimited shots of E&J on me.

To my in laws, hola.

Shareef stay real. As Salaammu Alaikum. Sha- Sheldon holler at your boy!
Malik thanks for the pep talks. They kept me going out for round two, battle after battle.
Fat Has I didn't forget you baby. Fat Qua, Ookie, Kenya, G, Lenny Buff, Terry (Wahid) Toot, Pop, Chewy, Lamar, Demond Davis, Big Ant, Lovey, Al Ski, Alex, Rashan (Buff) Little Bob, Rog Elder, Khattib, J. Lewis, Raheem Summers and Michael Cunningham "One Love." Hak, I see you. To all my peoples from G.K.V. stay up.
Jamie Lee, I represent the location (12th Ave. and 7th St) Holler!!

Big up to the entire hood, my cross-town cats, my up the hill cats, down the hill cats and my out of town cats.

Blood and Ozie ya'll refused to give me a job, I had to do something. (Ha, Ha, Ha)
Big shot out to TLE Variety on Central Avenue, Keystone Variety, Black Books and Horizon Books, thanks for pushing the book.

In addition I would like to thank my initial readers for spreading the word and introducing the book to other readers.

Whoa! I almost forgot the "HATERS." When will ya'll learn? Your hate only motivates me! Thanks for hating, Luv Ya (Ha, Ha, Ha)

And last but not least, I have to thank the game for giving me the insight to write this book.

Words for the wise to all the players, playing in these wicked streets:
Play the game. Don't let the game play you. Find your EXIT before the clock stops, and the screen reads GAME OVER. Peace!!!!!!!!!!!!!

TRUE 2 LIFE PRODUCTIONS
Order Form

True 2 Life Productions
P.O.BOX 8722
Newark, N.J. 07108

E-mail: true2lifeproductions@verizon.net
Website: www.true2lifeproductions.com

SINCERELY YOURS ?
ISBN # 0-974-0610-2-6 $13.95
Sales Tax (6% NJ)   .83
Shipping/ Handling
Via U.S. Priority Mail $ 3.85
Total $18.63

Also by the Author:
Block Party
ISBN # 0-974-0610-1-8 $14.95
Sales Tax (6% NJ)   .89
Shipping/Handling
Via U.S. Priority Mail $3.85
Total $19.69

No Exit
ISBN # 0-974-0610-0-X $13.95
Sales Tax (6% NJ)   .83
Shipping/ Handling
Via U.S. Priority Mail $ 3.85
Total $18.63

PURCHASER INFORMATION

Name: _____

Address: _____

City: _____ State: _____ Zip Code: _____

Sincerely Yours? ____

Block Party ____

No Exit ____

HOW MANY BOOKS? _____

Make checks/money orders payable to:
True 2 Life Productions